Under the sea . . .

Marina looked across the broad flat back of the whale shark's body and gently touched its side. She drew her hand back at the surprising coarse sandpaper texture. It looked so smooth!

The shark must have been five or six feet wide. There were several sharklike remora fish no more than a foot or so long attached to the underside of the whale shark. They slid around but stayed suckered on by their mouths—parasites waiting for a free meal. Rhee was on the other side flailing around and trying to stay upright while fiddling to get water out of her snorkel mask.

Marina ignored her and kicked farther up and over the checked pattern of stripes and spots across the whale shark's three back ridges to inspect the small eye on the side of its head. She laughed out loud in delight, sending a plume of water shooting out of her snorkel tube. She was underwater. In the Caribbean. Looking into the eye of the biggest fish in the world! She grabbed Link's passing hand and squeezed it. She just had to share the high of the experience. His mouth grinned around the snorkel mouthpiece, and together they kicked up the length of the shark. Her body was tingling from snorkel tube to fin tip.

Girl Overboard

Aimee Ferris

speak

An Imprint of Penguin Group (USA) Inc.

Acknowledgments

I wish to acknowledge the assistance of my agent, John Silbersack; the hard work of my editor, Angelle Pilkington; the friendship of writing buds, Lindsey Leavitt and Luisa Plaja; the people of Roatan for allowing me to call their island home in every sense of the word; and the unending love and support of my grandparents, Maggie and Donnie Ferris, who taught me to take things as they come, but believed those things would eventually include: Nobel Peace Prizes, Oscars, Emmys, Pulitzer Prizes, the cover of Vogue, *stars on the Hollywood Walk of Fame, art exhibits at MoMA, extended runs as a female lead on Broadway, winning lottery tickets . . .*

SPEAK
Published by the Penguin Group
Penguin Group (USA) Inc., 345 Hudson Street, New York, New York 10014, U.S.A.
Penguin Group (Canada), 90 Eglinton Avenue East, Suite 700, Toronto, Ontario, Canada M4P 2Y3
(a division of Pearson Penguin Canada Inc.)
Penguin Books Ltd, 80 Strand, London WC2R 0RL, England
Penguin Ireland, 25 St Stephen's Green, Dublin 2, Ireland
(a division of Penguin Books Ltd)
Penguin Group (Australia), 250 Camberwell Road, Camberwell, Victoria 3124, Australia
(a division of Pearson Australia Group Pty Ltd)
Penguin Books India Pvt Ltd, 11 Community Centre, Panchsheel Park,
New Delhi - 110 017, India
Penguin Group (NZ), 67 Apollo Drive, Mairangi Bay, Auckland 1311,
New Zealand (a division of Pearson New Zealand Ltd)
Penguin Books (South Africa) (Pty) Ltd, 24 Sturdee Avenue, Rosebank,
Johannesburg 2196, South Africa

Registered Offices: Penguin Books Ltd, 80 Strand, London WC2R 0RL, England

Published by Speak, an imprint of Penguin Group (USA) Inc., 2006

3 5 7 9 10 8 6 4

Copyright © Aimee Ferris, 2007
All rights reserved
Interior art and design by Jeanine Henderson. Text set in Imago Book.

LIBRARY OF CONGRESS CATALOGING-IN-PUBLICATION DATA
Ferris, Aimee.
Girl overboard / by Aimee Ferris.
p.   cm.—(S.A.S.S.)
Summary: Marina joins a group of international teens for a semester at sea in the Caribbean,
learning about marine life and resolving some issues about her relationships and her future.
SPEAK ISBN: 978-0-14-240799-8
[1. Foreign study—Fiction. 2. Marina animals—Fiction. 3. Interpersonal relations—Fiction.
4. Caribbean Area—Fiction.] I. Title.
PZ7.F3737Gi 2007 [Fic]—dc22 2006030624

Printed in the United States of America

With love to Nakoa—the best island boy of all.

Girl Overboard

Marina's
Tiburon Yacht

KEY:

Stairs
Computer Room
Photo Room
Equipment Lockers
Sun Deck
Marina's Room

UPPER DECK

MIDDLE DECK

Cabin

Cabin

Cabin

Cabin

Cabin

Captain's
Cabin

Kitchen

Lounge

Dining Area

Bathroom

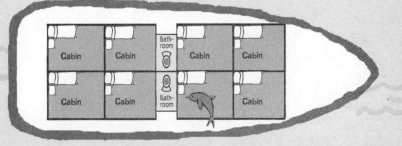

Cabin

Cabin

Bath-
room

Cabin

Cabin

Cabin

Cabin

Bath-
room

Cabin

LOWER DECK

Application for the Students Across the Seven Seas
Study Abroad Program

Name: Marina Grey

Age: 17

High School: Village of Stowe High School

Hometown: Stowe, Vermont

Preferred Study Abroad Destination: Caribbean Semester at Sea

1. Why are you interested in traveling abroad next year?

Answer: To expand my horizons before moving 3,000 miles away from family and friends to pursue a degree in marine biology at the University of Hawaii.

(Truth: I need to find out if my dream career or my boyfriend are more important to my future happiness, and if it will be a dealbreaker one way or the other.)

2. How will studying abroad further develop your talents and interests?

Answer: I have pursued every connection to the marine world I could while in Vermont. Though I've learned a lot, the local fish hatchery is limited in what it can teach me about the greater field of marine biology.

(Truth: I need to see if I can break away from the life I know and concentrate on the life I want, or if I can combine the two somehow without it all falling apart. I think the only way to sort out my emotions is to get away and see how things go.)

3. Describe your extracurricular activities.

Answer: Skiing, volunteering at the fish hatchery, hiking in the Green Mountains

(Truth: Skiing, volunteering at the fish hatchery, hiking in the Green Mountains, and spending as much time as I can with my boyfriend)

4. Is there anything else you feel we should know about you?

Answer: I am passionate about marine biology—especially in relation to dolphins—and I hope to one day work in the field.

(Truth: I hope I don't get so homesick for my boyfriend that I want to run home the minute after I get out on the boat.)

Chapter One

Marina cringed as her monstrous purple suitcase slid down the baggage ramp and landed with a sickening thud on top of a small carry-on. A petite girl standing next to Marina wailed in dismay.

As the travelers crowding the baggage claim in Miami International struggled to help free the girl's little mushed bag from under the purple hulk, Marina Grey surveyed the situation and decided to sit tight and let her mother's idea of stylish luggage make a second round of the corral.

One perk of being several thousand miles south of her Vermont hometown was that no one knew her name. This

happened to be a good thing since "Marina" was engraved along with three jumping dolphins on the silver handle of the embarrassing bag. As it came back around, she took a deep breath and hauled the suitcase up.

Standing on tiptoes, she tried to locate the Students Across the Seven Seas contact person, but Miami International was packed with people dressed in gaudy fluorescent sundresses and Hawaiian shirts. March in Vermont was still three-feet-of-snow-on-the-ground freezing. But her plane mates had scattered, leaving her a lone stretch-cord-jeans-and-boots fish in a sea of flip-flops.

"Fish out of water," she mumbled. "Great, I've officially become a cliché."

A group of tourists in matching "his and her" hot pink shirts and muumuus surrounded her, and she felt the sudden uncomfortable sensation of being hijacked by a flock of overweight flamingos. She rose on her toes again. For once, she was grateful for her five feet eleven inches as she spotted a man in a bright orange S.A.S.S. polo. She pushed up her long sleeves and picked her way through the crowd, almost panting from the effort.

"Marina?" asked a deep voice through the whitest smile she had ever seen.

The guy was right out of the fashion mags: jet black hair, tanned skin, broad shoulders; he was even *tall*.

Marina dragged her eyes away from him and tried not

to blush. He reached for her suitcase, and she almost forgot to let go of the handle. With a second tug and a smile, he lifted it up and put it on the trolley on top of two nearly identical streamlined black backpacks.

"Did you know that your mouth is hanging open?" said a heavily accented French girl standing beside the S.A.S.S. adviser. Her glossy dark hair was pulled back into a casual twist that had probably taken her two seconds to put up. Marina had tried the look once but ended up only with cramped arms and a mess of long, blonde tangles. She had stuck to braids after that.

The thin blonde next to the French girl snickered at the obvious comment. Marina snapped her mouth shut and gave up the useless fight not to blush. She stared at her boots instead.

"Er, how did you know I'm Marina?" she stammered at the ground.

"Well, unless you answer to Lincoln and are a white-water-raft guide from Australia, you'd pretty much have to be Marina." He smiled.

"Right. Then, yes, I would be Marina." She attempted a smile back.

Marina had spent the plane trip convincing herself it was okay to leave the old version of herself behind. After so many years coasting, knowing everyone in her tiny town and their knowing her, it was time to start fresh. She could do first impressions. No problem. She pulled herself up

and smiled again with confidence. "What's your name?" Marina asked as he handed her his clipboard to sign.

"Marco. I'm the program adviser, and also one of the instructors."

She looked up and stared. One dimple. The guy had one dimple. It was simply too much. That one dimple doomed her to a whole new kind of cliché—crush-on-the-teacher cliché. The worst.

"Oh. 'Marco' is Spanish, right?" she asked with some effort.

"*Italiano*, actually," Marco said.

"Not everyone in Miami is Hispanic, you know," said the blonde girl in a thick southern drawl.

She and the French girl sidled up to each other. One nudged the other and murmured something at which they both giggled. These two were going to be trouble, Marina could tell already.

"Well, half Italian, half Dominican. My mother's from the Dominican Republic," he added with a wink for Marina.

At the wink, Marina felt one knee buckle. Not both knees, just one. This was good; she could control a one-knee-buckling crush. And a nice harmless crush on an instructor—a very young instructor—could distract her from dwelling on her boyfriend, Damon, the whole time.

She and Damon had been inseparable for three years. Their friends had even given them the annoying nickname "Damarina." She loved Damon but tended to be of the opinion that a girl deserved her own name. And Damon had not been pleased at this latest escapade of hers. "Why do you have to go away to figure out us?" he had asked. Breaking the news that she was going to be studying abroad on a six-week program at sea, and why, had not been easy to explain.

There were the obvious reasons. She had been nearly obsessed with dolphins and all sea life since going to Sea World when she was eight. She had been the audience participant during the show, and the minute the dolphin snatched the little fish from her hand, something clicked. Even her name—what could "Marina" mean but that she was destined to become a marine biologist?

Dreaming of becoming the next Jackie Cousteau was not very practical in Vermont, but Marina did what she could. She volunteered at the Northern Vermont Fish Hatchery to soak up knowledge from the biologists about fish and sea life. She spent idle hours just sitting, digging her toes in the chilly sand and staring at massive Lake Champlain. It was hardly the sea, but a land-locked girl had to make do. So when she saw the S.A.S.S. sign for the Caribbean Study Adventure with a marine biology focus and stops in the Bahamas, Bay Islands, and the Dominican Republic, it was a no-brainer.

But this was Damon, her best friend and near constant companion since freshman year. He knew all of those things but would look right through them and see the doubt in her eyes. Things had been rocky between them lately. So besides the whole once-in-a-lifetime, amazing-tropical-experience reason for going, what could she say without seeming like a horrible person? I'm sorry your mom got sick, and I know why you want to stay in Vermont, but I need to figure out if I'm okay with *your* family situation changing *our* plans? I need to find out which is more awful—going away *without* you, or staying *with* you but being stuck in this small town forever? I can't even tell if I still love you or if we rely on each other so much that you're my safety net to help me make it in the world?

Scratch that last one. That one's way too scary. After all, that particular safety net had puppy dog brown eyes that crinkled when he smiled and wore her favorite cologne even though he hated it and... uh-oh. The beautiful Dominican-Italian teacher had been talking to her while she was lost in her imaginary conversation with her boyfriend.

"—is Natalia from Louisiana and Rheanna from France, both also with the S.A.S.S. program. Lincoln is from Australia and is joining us through another organization."

They all turned to survey the crowd, trying to pick out someone who looked like an Australian "Lincoln." Maybe he'd be wearing a stove-pipe hat with one side of the brim folded up.

As she watched the masses of tromping cruise goers following a sombrero'ed Fiesta Line representative, she was glad she'd be on a boat with only fifteen other students and crew instead of thousands like some of the ships boasted. The sleek lines and tinted windows of the *Tiburon* on her brochure looked more like it housed the champagne-and-caviar set than the all-you-can-eat-buffet set.

Marina eyed the two new boat mates standing next to her with suspicion. The girls were wearing almost identical black capris with white strappy tanks and sandals. When she looked closer, the blonde girl's pants looked like they had started out long and were just rolled up. Her tank also had a little insignia that said Miami, as if she had bought it at the airport gift shop. Did Marina miss a memo about a required uniform? Maybe they were Stepford students. That whole "pulled together" look was so impossible for Marina, she couldn't even manage to work up a proper bit of jealousy over it.

She stifled a giggle as they compared their matching giant movie-star sunglasses. These were S.A.S.S. girls though, so they had to be all right. The screening process was pretty comprehensive; both social and educational aspects were covered. Maybe she misread their attitude—different cultures or something. She'd never been to the South, other than the one trip to Florida when she was little. She held out her hand and tried again.

"Hi, I'm Marina."

"Rhee."

"Tali."

Tali imitated Rhee's bored tone. They proceeded to ignore her, craning their necks trying to spot Lincoln. Rhee actually reached out and grabbed Marina's arm, moving her to one side to get a better look for the new arrival. Marina bristled. She was deciding how to respond when she saw Tali's eyes widen and heard her gasp. She spun around to see a vision in surf shorts heading their way.

Out of the crowd sauntered a buff, shaggy-haired guy. Glancing around, his eyes fell on Marco and then instantly slid to the three girls. He smiled a lazy smile. The girls were frozen in place. Marina was the first to break.

"No way," she breathed, grateful Damon wasn't there to see her new boat mate.

"Way!" yelped Tali.

Rhee's long fingernails dug into Marina's upper arm. Marina pried them loose and flinched at Rhee's hiss.

"Le mien!"

She didn't need French 101 to understand a girl staking her claim on a guy. "Catty" was a universal language.

Marina looked from Marco to the stranger now signing the clipboard and shook her head. She wondered if maybe every place outside of Vermont was full of guys who could pose for Abercrombie ads. She certainly didn't care much about fashion, and neither did her friends. For a state that spent half the year in knit hats, often complete with earflaps, the world of hair gel would forever remain a mystery, and she was okay with that. Maybe this was just what the rest of the world looked like.

"Lincoln here; call me Link."

Boom, there went the other knee. That Aussie accent. He lightly tossed his huge duffel onto the baggage trolley and turned to the girls.

"G'day, sheilas!"

Marina's giggle ended in a small snort. Arggh. This always happened when she was nervous. She hoped others found it an endearing quality. Her mom assured her they did. But then again, mothers weren't always the best ones to believe in these matters.

Link was looking straight into Marina's eyes with his head cocked. At least he wasn't taller than her, just exactly even. Maybe she would make it out of this airport without a wheelchair yet. She was glad they weren't picking up any other guys, though. She was entirely kneeless as it was.

"Sorry, I didn't mean to laugh. I'm Marina. It's just, well, do you really talk like that?" she asked.

Link stepped close, invading her personal space. Marina tried to feel invaded but failed. He reached out to play with the blonde wisps at the end of her thick braid.

"Marina," he whispered to himself.

He tossed her braid back over her shoulder and flashed a mischievous smile. "Look more like a Barbie to me."

He had already moved on to appraise the other girls,

and, try as she might, Marina couldn't hold in her lifelong habit of making bad puns.

"Suppose you'll be throwing another shrimp on me, then."

Link paused midflirt with Rhee, who did not look pleased at the interruption, and laughed. "Oh, this is gonna be a good trip." He caught her eye with a nod...and winked.

Unbelievable. Seventeen years of winkless existence goes by, and here she was, a mere half hour off the plane and double-blasted. This was the sort of thing you'd tell a girlfriend. If you had one, instead of spending all your time with your boyfriend, that is. She had a feeling that Damon wouldn't find that little factoid entertaining.

Marina's thoughts were interrupted by Marco's voice.

"'Kay. Looks like we've got everybody now. Let's head to the yacht!"

The S.A.S.S. van cruised through the strip on South Beach, with Marco acting as tour guide. Art deco hotels in various pastel colors lined one side of the road, while nearly naked model-type girls lined the beach on the other. Link was sitting up front next to Marco and nudged him.

"You can leave me right here, mate. Catch up with you guys in May!"

Marina was pleased to see Marco deflect the cheap guy-guy remark.

"Wait until we get you under the sea, Link; then you will

see nature's real beauty. Most of this is man-made."

"Marco's soooo deep," Tali whispered to Rhee from the backseat.

Marina decided she would need some serious pain medication if she had to be in close range of airhead Tali for much longer. Her eyes already ached from their near constant need to roll while in the girl's presence. But she did have a point about Marco. Marina decided to devote half of Link's knee-buckle over to Marco's side. Link would be altogether annoying if it weren't for that accent.

She looked behind her at the girls to see if they were both listening to the guys' conversation. Rhee didn't appear to mind Link's attitude a bit. She was taking in his every movement with narrowed eyes. Marina had seen that same look in one of those animal programs about snakes sizing up their prey. She briefly considered offering Rhee a Kleenex to wipe off the drool.

"How far is it to the dock?" Link asked.

"Oh, about four and a half miles," Marco said.

"Ah, miles. I've got my head stuck in kliks and the metric system."

"Oui," Rhee said, with obvious disdain for American miles. She'd probably agree with anything Link said, though.

"Klik? What's that?" Tali asked.

"It's an abbreviation for kilometer," Marina said. She better get used to explaining things to this flaky—

"Oh. Well, one klik, or kilometer, equals about 0.6213 miles, right? So about 7.2405 kilometers to the boat—ooh, check it out!" Tali squealed. She pointed at a girl in a gold chain bikini and heels walking three miniature poodles, each of which was wearing a little gold sun visor.

Marina leaned out the window a bit. The dogs didn't have matching heels, but she wouldn't have been surprised if they did. She sat back, still stunned at Tali's calculation. "Wait. How did you do that?" Marina asked.

Tali leaned forward over the back of Marina's seat and looked at her blankly for a minute. "Well, I guess it would make more sense for us to think of it as one mile equaling 1.609 kilometers. You know, since we are used to miles and everything—"

"All these numbers bore me. Just get us to the boat so we can wash off the American airport smell," Rhee said.

Tali slid back in the seat under Rhee's disapproving glare.

"That's cool you could do that in your head," Marina said to Tali.

"Guess math is just my thing."

Rhee mumbled something under her breath, and Tali giggled. Marina knew they were talking about her again. She sighed and redirected her attention to the passing sights and sounds. They were leaving behind the last sidewalk café of people-watchers and people-to-be-watched, and were heading toward the highway.

They passed the massive cruise ship docks and a sign that read KEY BISCAYNE. The official S.A.S.S. letter mentioned their yacht was docked in a place called Coconut Grove. It sounded too romantic to be the name of a real town, but perfect for a place from which to start an adventure.

As the van pulled into the marina's parking area, even Rhee seemed to drop her air of affected boredom and sat up to look. Row upon row of expensive-looking, glowing white boats filled the docks. Marco pulled up in front of the largest of the boats and stopped the van.

"Welcome to your new home!"

Chapter Two

Marina had no trouble tearing her eyes away from Marco's smile now. The white mini-cruise ship looked even more glamorous in person than on the brochure. Long and sleek, with tinted windows that gave the impression that some celeb should be inside, hiding from the paparazzi. She couldn't believe it was real.

Marco explained that the yacht was brand-new, on loan from the famous Tiburon fleet in exchange for the crew delivering the boat to its new home in the Dominican Republic. Completely outfitted for a week at sea, the boat would take recreational divers on luxury cruises with a four-star chef preparing the meals, diving expeditions up to five times a day, and heated towels available postdive. And it was theirs for six weeks!

Marina stared through the window and waited for the boat to dissolve like a mirage. But there it was. She was really going to do this. She had thought that at this moment she'd be suave. She thought she'd be clever. She thought she'd be sophisticated...she hadn't thought she'd be nauseous. She jumped with a nervous giggle as Marco appeared before her and slid open the van door.

"Something funny?" he asked.

"No. I was just thinking how much I'm already learning about myself," Marina said with a smile.

"This will do," sniffed Rhee, pushing past Marina to be first out of the van.

Marina ignored her and climbed out onto the dock. A steady stream of "Get out!"s, "Shut up!"s flew from Tali's mouth. Marina didn't want to be rude, but she sort of wished the girl would do both. Tali's dramatics were making her even jumpier.

She was about to spend two whole months on this boat. This wasn't Camp Ondesonkian, where she made it through only four days before calling to go home. But next year was senior year, and after that she'd be on her own for real. Or maybe she'd be at home with Damon. She needed to figure things out. And what a gorgeous place to live while she did. She shielded her eyes from the sun

that sparkled off the white decks of the boat. The echo of seagulls and surf helped to wipe away any lingering doubts, and she grinned in spite of herself.

Tali flung herself out of the van and grabbed Rhee and Marina's hands while jumping up and down. Marina softened a little and made a mental note to stop lumping the two girls together in the same icky place in her mind. Maybe Tali would be all right away from Rhee. Annoying, but not awful.

Marco walked up the shifting boat ramp first and offered a hand to help them across the space between the side of the boat and the dock. Marina clung to the flimsy ramp rail and wondered how she was going to get her bag onto the yacht. Visions of falling overboard and float-ing away at sea on an ugly purple raft filled her head. She gave a sigh of relief when she saw members of the boat crew unloading the van.

"It'll take a few days to get used to the sway," Marco said, noticing Marina's wary look. "Won't be bad in port, which is where you'll be most of the time. I'll give you a brief tour, but your orientation will be tomorrow morn-ing since one of our students won't make it in until late tonight."

They followed Marco across the back deck, which was packed with tidy sets of dive equipment. She'd taken her diving course in chilly, dark Lake Champlain. There wasn't much sea life, but one time she did see an Oldsmobile on the bottom. She couldn't wait to dive the colorful fish-filled reefs of the warm Caribbean.

Marco pointed to the left and right of a staircase down to the lower deck. "Heads, aka bathrooms, toilets, restrooms, washrooms. There are two with showers here. Only a few cabins have bathrooms inside, and those are on the upper deck and belong to the crew and your instructors. These heads are for student use."

"I'm sorry—did you say there were only two bathrooms? For all of us?" Tali was showing the first signs of panic.

"Perfectly normal. Remember, this boat will be used for regular paying guests and they don't seem to have a problem with it. It's all a part of life on the sea."

"And a great way to meet your boat mates," Link teased.

"There's one extra bathroom, no shower, down here in the lounge area," Marco continued.

Marco was walking down the stairs into the lower deck. Marina followed and was surprised at what a cozy area they had to hang out in. Big fluffy sofas lined the walls, and a plasma TV was in one corner in front of a work table full of video equipment. The thick carpeted floor was sunken, and there were bunches of pillows lying around. Large underwater photos of sharks, eels, and octopi covered the walls.

Marco walked across the carpet and stepped up into the dining area. There was a large round booth on the side

of the L-shaped kitchen counter and two other cafeteria tables across the aisle. Everything was bolted down.

"The deck above me has the student cabins. There are eight, and you may pair up as you choo—"

"I'm with Rhee!" Tali blurted, hugging her new friend's arm.

Rhee gave Marina a smug smile.

"Sorry, Marina," Rhee said sweetly.

"Then I'm bunking with Barbie!" said Lincoln.

"What! I don't think so—" Marina started.

"Hold on, hold on. No co-eds. We're not going there. Tali and Rhee, go ahead up and see what cabins are left; several people have already chosen. Doors should all be ope—"

The girls were already racing up the stairs, Rhee whispering and Tali giggling her head off, no doubt discussing how to snag the best available cabin. Marina didn't care; she was starting to warm up to the idea of this being her new home.

"Oh, sorry, Barbie. Are you disappointed?" Link teased.

"I think I'll get over it, thanks."

Marco looked at his clipboard. "Actually, looks like you are the last of the guys, Link. I imagine your cabinmate is probably in the photo room." He headed over to what appeared to be a closet door and knocked. A distracted voice filtered out.

"It's open."

Marco opened the door. Inside the tiny room they could see the back of someone leaning over a photo slide tray with a magnifying glass.

"This is Ryan; he's American."

"Actually, I'm from Canada," Ryan explained in a resigned voice without looking up.

Marina pulled at the thighs of her cords, which were sticking to her in the uncomfortable heat. At least she wasn't the only one who hadn't thought through her traveling outfit, she noted, seeing Ryan's heavy hiking boots.

"Right. Sorry. Your cabinmate has arrived. Ryan, this is Link."

"Hey." He turned to shake hands.

Well, finally, Marina thought. A normal-looking person. With his anonymous white T-shirt and ball cap pulled down so low you could hardly see his eyes, Ryan could even pass for a Vermonter. The image was completed when he straightened up to shake hands, and she saw the plaid long-sleeve shirt tied around the waist of his jeans.

She had come dangerously close to wearing an almost identical outfit today. The T-shirt had been one of those fitted ones, but other than that... Well, she was just glad she'd decided it looked too lumberjacky.

"Um, Marco?"

"Whatcha need, Marina?"

"I am dying to get out of these clothes."

Marina blushed at Link's loud laugh. She then quickly

corrected herself. "I mean, could I go on up and find my cabin?"

Marina took in her new room. It was tiny, but everything she could possibly need was there, only in miniature form. Sitting on the bottom bunk was "Dude," the bright blue stuffed dolphin Damon had given her as a going-away present. A touch of home. She felt a bit guilty for taking the lower bunk and leaving the upper for the mystery girl, but who knew when her roommate would arrive. And Marina was still getting used to the sway of the boat and wanted to be closer to the floor, where she was sure to land at some point in the night.

She looked out the tiny porthole. The boat was docked, so all she was able to see was the walkway and other boats, but even that was exciting. Row after row of bright white yachts gleamed in the late-afternoon sun. There were well-dressed people on the decks of some of them having well dressed-drinks with their well-dressed friends. It all looked so perfectly glamorous.

And then something not so perfect marred the view. Rhee seemed to be leading Tali and a group of the other students down the dock like royalty. Marina'd seen that sort of girl in movies and read about her in books, but she hadn't ever had to deal with such cliquiness herself.

At her school, with a junior class of only sixty-three, no one with Rhee's haughty attitude would have lasted a day—mostly because all the students had grown up together. It's hard to feel superior to someone when you know their parents probably have a picture of you in diapers. That made her relationship with Damon all the more special. With his having moved to Stowe, Vermont, during their freshman year, he was probably the only guy she could have dated without it feeling incestuous.

She counted the students heading down the dock with Rhee. Looked like about twelve were there. So basically the whole boat. Nice. She would like to think it was because she was in her cabin that no one had come to get her, but she wondered if Rhee and Tali had just "forgotten" her on purpose.

With the group was Teresa, a nice girl from Aspen she'd run into earlier while she waited for the shower. When she had introduced herself, she pronounced her name in the Spanish way, Te-ray-sa, but the rest of her speech didn't have the slightest bit of an accent. They'd talked East vs. West skiing for a while, but Marina changed the subject when thoughts of Damon crept in. She didn't think tearing up would make a good first impression.

Marco had given them the night for free time to pick up last-minute trip items and have a dinner out in Coconut Grove. They just had to go in groups, and sign out and back in. She wandered down to the lounge to check the sign-out list to see if anyone was left onboard.

The heat hit her as she walked down the steps. It felt

so good she couldn't wait to throw on her suit and lay out with a good book. If she went to her dream school, the University of Hawaii, she'd be able to do that all the time. The thought made her smile.

She traced the list of students with her finger. There were only four empty boxes. Hers, Ryan's, Link's, and some girl named Jeanette, who was presumably her cabinmate. Well, Jeanette wasn't arriving until later, and she sure wasn't going to approach Link to go out. His bordering-on-sleazy flirting was almost comical, but the fact that it was done by a gorgeous guy with a killer accent made her leery. It was hard not to like the attention, ridiculous as it was. Maybe Ryan would be up for a meal. She felt sort of weird having dinner with some strange guy, but Ryan seemed cool. He felt like home somehow.

She scanned the sign-out list again. Someone had written their cabin numbers next to their names. So it wasn't a case of the group not being able to find her. Marina's face burned at the thought. She didn't care about Tali or Rhee, but she'd hoped Teresa and the others on the boat would have been nicer than that. She had seen some guys and other girls roaming around earlier, checking out the boat in small groups. She hoped they didn't take her shyness the wrong way. After living in a small town like Stowe, it was hard to be in a place where you didn't know a soul. She went to the darkroom to find Ryan, but her knock went unanswered.

Marina stared at the floor and wondered for the thirty-second time that day whether she'd made the right decision to come. This was not starting out to be much fun. Before she could come to any conclusions, she noticed that the white tile under her feet was cast with an orange glow, and she walked over to the window to see what was causing it. The sight had her running up the stairs to the deck. She stood at the railings with the warm breeze blowing through her still damp hair and gaped. The world was turning pink and purple and orange and red, and she had never seen anything like it. They had nice sunsets that they could view from the top of the ski slope in Vermont, but they looked distant. This sun seemed to completely envelop her in a blur of colors. She held her breath without even realizing it.

A feeling of utter contentment seeped with the warmth into her skin, and she sighed. This was where she was meant to be at that very moment, and nothing, not even a twosome of snotty girls, would spoil it.

Chapter Three

Marina was still staring out at the pink and gold rays when she felt a hand on the small of her back. She nearly jumped out of her nice warm skin. Seeing the hand attached to the arm of none other than Link did nothing to reassure her.

"Hey, Barbie, did ya miss me?"

"Yes. Those few hours apart were really tough, but somehow I made it through."

Link laughed but didn't move his hand. The warmth was anything but comfortable on those few inches of her back.

"Beautiful."

She turned back to the purpley orange glow and had to agree.

"It is. It's like nothing I've ever seen before."

"Oh, the sunset. Well that, too. I was talking about your stems."

She looked up to see him staring at her legs. Her stems? Where on earth did this guy learn his moves? He was such a cheeseball.

Her stomach growled suddenly, and she blushed at the loud grumble. Maybe he hadn't heard. Didn't stomach growls always sound louder in your own head?

"Hungry, are we? Can I buy you dinner?"

"No, I'm fine."

"Ah, so you're not hungry?"

Her stomach growled again.

"Well, yes. I'm hungry. But I just want to hang out and get a feel for the place."

She was making excuses, but as the words left her mouth, she realized that's exactly what she wanted to do. Tali and Rhee had sort of done her a favor.

"Well, I'm kicking myself for missing a night out in Coconut Grove, but even I am not invincible. That twenty-one-hour flight almost did me in, and I can't have my first impression on this lot be of someone as wrecked as I feel, can I?"

"Oh, I'm sure there are several of them who would welcome your company, wrecked or not."

Link leaned in and whispered, "That's just cause those sheilas are too easily impressed."

First the winking thing, now whispering in her ear? Link finally moved his hand away from her back and walked toward the lounge.

Marina breathed a sigh of relief.

"I like more of a challenge, myself," he called back.

Relief gone. That guy made her nervous. She'd just left her boyfriend behind twelve hours ago, and while things weren't exactly peachy keen in Damarina-land, she wasn't the sort of girl to go drooling after the first set of devastatingly ripped abs that walked by.

Was she? She didn't think so. Not that there were all that many devastatingly ripped sets of abs walking in and out of her life. She hoped she hadn't misjudged herself to be a cool, calm, collected sort of person, only to find out it was because her life thus far was devoid of any interesting temptations.

She sighed as the sun seemed to hover above the horizon and then finally slid into the ocean. Her stomach growled again. She walked back up to her cabin. Maybe she had a granola bar or something left in her carry-on.

Forty minutes later, as she was flipping through the program outline folder that had been left on their bunks, she heard a knock. She jumped up and brushed away the granola crumbs. She headed for the door and then ran back to push Dude under her bedspread so her new roommate wouldn't think she was totally immature.

"Jeanette" was a nice-sounding name. Hopefully the girl would be just as nice. She took a deep breath and opened the door with a smile.

"Hey, Barbie."

Her smile slid away like the sun. "You again." Marina didn't care if she sounded rude. Time to nip this thing in the bud. Her subtle hints that she wasn't interested were being ignored. On purpose, too, she gathered.

"Yep, brought you some tea."

"Thanks, I don't really drink tea—"

"No, some dinner, some grub. Aussies just call it tea."

Link held up two white plastic foam containers. He was holding two cans of Coke in the other hand.

Great. Now she felt bad for being rude. This must be yet another attempt to break down her walls so he could . . . well, she wasn't sure. But he didn't seem the type to be going to all this effort without some ulterior motive. The food smelled amazing, but she had the urge to see if there was an Alice in Wonderland sort of tag on the dish. Considering this was Link's doing, maybe her boobs would grow three sizes bigger if she ate it. Her thoughts must have been visible on her face.

"Go ahead. It's not poisoned."

"Sorry. I mean, thank you. You didn't have to." She took the container and Coke and started to close her door.

"Hang on! I thought..."

She paused and waited for him to finish.

"Well, I made up a table on the upper deck. The stars are coming out, and I thought maybe you'd ... but if you're too busy, it's fine. I can just..."

For the first time that day, he seemed uncertain. It was such an ill-fitting attitude for him that it was painful to see. She caved just to make it go away.

"Oh. Um, sure, that's fine."

She followed him along the deck to a side table set between two chaise lounges. The area was warmly lit by purple and blue Japanese lanterns strung along the rails, reflecting down on the sea. It was a great little spot along-side the captain's cabin. Probably where the instructors hung out, Marina decided. But it was deserted now.

"So where's Ryan?" she asked.

Link studied her for a moment before answering. "Dunno. Messing around with some camera stuff. Guess they have equipment here he's only read about in maga-zines. He's pretty into photography."

Marina took the cover off the container and the garlicy buttery scent of pasta hit her. She dove right in, the half-eaten granola bar forgotten.

"I ran into Marco when I left you. He was heading onto shore to pick up some takeout, so I tagged along. Didn't know what you liked, but looks like we have the same taste. And Marco seems like a cool guy. We had a long chat."

Marina nodded, pushing a loose strand of hair out of her face, and considered that she may have misjudged Link. It was nice of him to think of her. She wondered why he'd bothered. Then he got up and slid behind her on her chaise. Oh, that's why. He grabbed hold of her hair and started separating it into chunks.

"What are you doing?" she demanded.

"Braiding your hair. You do like it braided, don't you?"

He pulled the chunks tight and began twisting them around one another.

"Well, yes, but—" She took a deep breath. She was definitely annoyed, but she was also a severe bigtalkaphobe. If she wasn't such a wuss about things like this, she might have had some heart-to-hearts with Damon about their future, instead of just going with the flow and feeling confused about things all the time. But this whole Link thing needed to stop, and before anyone caught wind of it on the boat. She did not come two thousand miles to break away from being Damarina only to become Linkarina or Marinalink or Malinka or some other stupid combo that would suck away who she was right when she finally had the chance to figure it out. She tried to pull away, but he was still holding on to her hair. He tugged the still-wet hair band from her wrist and secured it.

"There."

She took another breath and turned to him.

"Okay, I don't want to be rude, but you need to listen up. I'm not into this, whatever this is. I think you're great and you know you're hot, but this won't work on me. I need to keep my head in my studies while I'm on board. I'm here to learn. Learn about marine biology and learn about being on my own. So no more dinners on the deck, no more braiding my hair, no more looking at my *stems*. I mean, do whatever you want, free country and all, but you're wasting your time if you think it's going anywhere."

She caught his brief look of disappointment before he plastered a cocky grin back on his face.

"So you're telling me that you don't feel a thing sitting here with me? No chemistry, no warm fuzzies?"

She looked him square in the eyes and lied. "No. Nothing."

He was quiet for a moment, and Marina cringed, figuring he'd be like every other guy and go on the offensive in the face of rejection.

He looked up and gave her a crooked smile. "Well. Okay then."

"Okay?"

"Sure. I can respect that. Thanks for being straight with me. You're a cool girl, Marina."

"Thanks."

"By the way, the braid thing? I just look after my little

sister, Jenny, a lot when my mom's working. I braid Jenny's hair all the time."

Watching his little sister as a favor to his mom? It wasn't exactly the sort of thing Marina expected from a guy like Link. "That's really nice of you," she said. She hoped the shock wasn't obvious in her tone.

"Not really. Hell of a lot easier to braid it than to try to get the rats' nest out later. That girl's a tomboy; she gets into everything."

An awkward moment passed between them.

"Soooo—" he said.

Marina groaned inside as his cocky smile reappeared.

"So...what?"

"So, this is kind of nice. I don't have to bother trying to impress you, so I don't need to hide how stupid I am. Some of the prerequisite marine biology basics are beyond me. Do you think you could give me a hand with the science stuff?"

Marina laughed, grateful for his lightening the mood.

"I doubt you're stupid, but sure, I'll help you study."

"Great! I'll go grab my books."

"Meet you down in the lounge."

Marina stopped in her cabin to grab her books and came across the giant Toblerone bar she'd picked up at the airport. Since he'd supplied dinner, at least she could offer something for dessert. She passed by the mirror and almost dropped the chocolate in shock at the sight of her

perfectly braided hair. She took a second look, but there it was. Little Jenny had quite the hairdressing brother.

Marina pulled Dude closer and rolled over in her bunk bed. The aroma of creamy sweet coffee made her nose twitch. She rubbed her eyes against Dude's dorsal fin until they opened enough to locate the coffee on the nightstand. Marina jolted awake as she saw she wasn't alone in the cabin. A petite freckled girl stood in front of the wall mirror putting on eyeliner. The girl's open mouth curved into a smile when she caught Marina staring.

"Good morning, Sunshine! I was going to wait for you to wake up before I turned the light on, but you were out cold!"

Marina managed a groggy shake of her head. She kicked her legs out from under the blankets and tried to sit up. It took a minute for her to figure out where she was. The heat flooded her face when she remembered she was still hugging Dude. She quickly set him back on her bunk bed.

"Hey, girl, just take your time coming to. Boats knock you out good with all the swaying. Constant motion does it, they say." She handed Marina the mug of coffee.

"Thanks."

"My name's Jeanette. And you're Marina. At least according to the list downstairs."

The girl was constant motion, and Marina struggled to snap out of her daze and focus on her.

"Ooooh, cute dolphin! That makes me feel so much better. I brought the giraffe my mom gave me when I was a baby, but I kept it in my suitcase in case you'd think I was dumb," Jeanette said.

Jeanette was holding out a threadbare floppy-necked giraffe. Marina looked down at Dude the Dolphin, with his bright blue fur and the little hole from where Damon had ripped off the price tag instead of cutting it. She shoved Damon's gift under the covers and changed the subject before Jeanette asked anything more about it. She had the sudden urge to keep a distinct separation between life at home and life on the boat. At least until she could sort through things privately and at her own speed.

"Cool giraffe. So, we're going to be roommates, huh?"

Marina was shooting for friendly and outgoing. But in comparison to Jeanette's chipper on steroids, she was hoping at least to reach coherent. It was nice of her to bring coffee. Maybe Jeanette had just had a few too many javas. Like six too many. Marina drank a slug of the coffee, which tasted like candy, and stood to stretch.

"Oh my God! You're so tall!"

Jeanette didn't say it in a mean way, but Marina was surprised it didn't bother her. She was usually sensitive about her height. She could actually look down onto Jeanette's head of wild red curls.

"Everything's relative isn't it," Marina said with a smile.

"I know, I know. I'm five feet even. Not quite five, to tell the truth, but five feet sounds way better than four feet eleven and a half."

They were polar opposites. Marina was all slim arms and legs that went nearly up to Jeanette's substantial chest. Jeanette was pure curves. And judging by the way she wore her tiny sarong and cropped T, she knew it, too.

"What time is it?" Marina asked.

"Time to get a move on, girl. Marco—who, may I just say, *yum*—is doing orientation in about twenty minutes. Wow, your hair is as long as you are tall! Want help doing it?"

What was it with everyone's fascination with her hair? Marina walked over and checked herself out in the mirror. Her hair was still tight in Link's neat braid.

"Isn't it already done?"

"Are you kidding? You cannot wear it like that—what a waste! You have gorgeous hair. I won't allow it."

"Um, okay. I guess. We're here for new experiences, right?"

Jeanette had already started to undo her braid.

"If I let my hair grow out, instead of falling down my back like yours, it'd turn into a giant red afro two feet tall. Hey, maybe that's not such a bad idea."

Jeanette stopped long enough to pull her own curls straight up and check the look in the mirror before laughing. Marina took advantage of the moment to take another swig of coffee before Jeanette dove back into doing her hair.

"This is so fun! I do my friends' makeup for special events—dances, bridesmaid gigs, and things. But it's more of a formal thing then. Too conservative for my taste," said Jeanette.

Marina glanced at Jeanette's pierced belly button displayed above eight inches of low-slung sarong material. She hid her smile wondering what qualified as "conservative" for this girl.

"There. Now makeup, and you're good to go."

"No way. I hate that stuff. I'm fine."

"Seriously, you don't wear *any*?" she asked. Jeanette pointed to her own expertly made-up eyes. "Don't worry, this sort of look is not for you. I'll go natural, just a touch of mascara, waterproof even. And a dab of berry-stain lip gloss."

"Okay, I guess. If you think it will look good and not fake."

Jeanette swiped mascara up Marina's top lashes, slid gloss on her lips, and smiled.

"Look, you do have lashes! They were just so white they were invisible."

Jeanette grabbed Marina and turned her to the mirror. Marina stood shocked at the stranger looking back. Link had made such a tight braid that, unwound, it left giant fluffy waves of blonde hair, which fanned out over both shoulders. She looked far more together now after five minutes of Jeanette's handiwork than when she had spent

hours at the salon before the Christmas Ball. She caught sight of Jeanette slipping on some beaded flip-flops with four-inch foam platforms, and shook her head.

"This is amazing. How did you do this?"

"You like?" Jeanette beamed.

Marina declined Jeanette's offered sarong and pulled on her swimsuit and surf shorts with a plain white T. Somehow the choice of lip gloss brought out the aqua blue of her eyes. Her new roommate definitely had a gift.

Marina picked up her coffee mug again just before Jeanette took her arm and pulled her down to the dining area. A bunch of the students were already sitting at tables or milling about. Link and Ryan were in the large round booth, and Link waved them over.

"Oh, my! Who's the hottie?" Jeanette asked as they walked over.

"Oh, that's just Link."

"Um, Marina? That guy is not a 'just' anything. You already got dibs?"

Marina looked down at Jeanette and laughed. This could be the perfect nail in the coffin of the dangerous flirtation with Link. Just in case she got weak and wavered.

"Nope, and know what? I think you two would hit it off. Bet you have a lot in common."

"In common? Who needs anything in common when he looks like that?"

"Good point."

Marina slid into the booth next to Ryan and introduced Jeanette.

"You look different, Marina," Ryan said.

He didn't say it as a compliment or an insult, and his tone made Marina uncomfortable.

"You look great. You both do. Who's your friend?" Link ogled Jeanette, who glowed back at him.

Marina found that once she got past the initial twinge of disappointment that Link had given up on her so easily, she didn't even mind him placing his attention on Jeanette. Now if it were Rhee or Tali, it would be a different story. Even being a player, he seemed too good for them. But if he liked challenges, she wasn't so sure Jeanette was his girl.

She noticed Ryan pick up his program manual and start reading with a smirk. He seemed to find his roommate's intentions as transparent as Marina did.

"Can I get you a coffee, Jeanette?" Link asked.

"Why, yes please, Link. Three cream, three sugar."

"I think that's a milkshake, not a coffee," he said.

"What can I say? I like my coffee how I like my men, hot and sweet," she said with a wink.

Marina sputtered into her mug while Link gave a surprised but very pleased laugh. Ryan put down his program manual and stared at Jeanette.

"What? That doesn't even make sense," Ryan said.

"Oh, I dunno. I think I got my meaning across very well," Jeanette replied, and giggled.

"You're terrible, Jeanette," Marina said.

"Can't a girl have a little fun?"

Link brought back the coffee and slid in next to Jeanette. Marina shook her head with a smile, and they all shifted over.

"Check out those two. They didn't waste any time." Jeanette pointed to a tall curly-haired guy and a slender girl grabbing a doughnut at the buffet table.

"What do you mean?" asked Marina.

"They're together. Neither one of them moves more than an inch from the other—as though if some part of them is not touching at all times the world will end."

"Awww, you're right. I think that's kind of sweet," Marina said.

Early days of life with Damon slid into her head. Could that kind of infatuation ever bounce back after it fizzled? There was a time when they had held hands constantly, even when wearing their thick gloves on the ski lift up the mountain. Marina tried to remember the last time they'd done that. It must have been before Damon's mom got diagnosed with breast cancer. Though she'd been in remission the past year, the shadow of such serious stuff made that sort of thing seem immature. After everything they'd been through, she knew she *loved* him more, but it was hard not to miss the *in love* part.

Jeanette rolled her eyes at Marina and made gagging faces, much to Link's amusement. They seemed to share the same sense of humor. Ryan glanced at the doughnut-eating couple then looked back down at his book.

"Like the anemone and the clownfish," Ryan noted.

"Huh?" Jeanette said.

Ryan shook his head without looking at her. He stared at the ceiling as if searching for the right words to explain.

"Like Nemo?" he offered.

"I *know* what a clownfish is," Jeanette shot back.

"They take care of each other; one needs the other to get by."

"We had a lot of those round the reefs in my stomping grounds," Link said.

Ryan looked at him with interest. "You live near the Great Barrier Reef?"

"Right on it, tiny town in the rain forest called Mission Beach. I'm a raft guide on the Tully River there, but we all learned to scuba in school. We get out on the reef a few times a month."

"You're a raft guide? That sounds awesome," Jeanette said.

"It is. Miss it already. But I need to go back to school. I fluffed up my senior year, so taking this course is getting me a pass into university."

Marina noticed the couple looking for two spots together in the now-crowded dining area. Two smaller rectangular tables across the narrow aisle each seated five. Teresa was deep in conversation with two guys at the

head of one table, and the other was filled with five students with what sounded like five different accents lively discussing Bob Marley's music. Their round booth next to the L-shaped kitchen counter seated six, and since there were two spaces left, she smiled and gave a little half wave to the couple. Better to be joined by the clownfish/anemone than to get stung by the Mean Girls.

"Hey, can we sit with you guys?" the girl asked.

Marina recognized the girl's subtle New York accent from the many weekend tourists who came to Vermont to hit the slopes. Ryan moved back to make room and gave Marina a shy smile as they brushed legs.

"More the merrier," said Jeanette.

"Thanks, we were having a chat and lost track of time," the guy said in an accent similar to Link's.

"Oh, no way! You telling me I come all the way to the Caribbean, and I'm stuck with a sheep shagger?" Link burst out.

Marina's jaw dropped, but the guy just laughed and offered his hand.

"Now, you know the idea that New Zealanders have such close relationships to their livestock is nothing more than a nasty rumor. Not like the historical fact that England populated Australia with their unwanted prisoners, right, mate?" The guy shook Link's hand with a laugh. "So, if you can handle sitting down with a sheep lover, I can handle breaking bread with a convict."

Link clapped the guy on his back, and they sat down. Marina smiled. With all the different accents floating in the air, it was like being on a U.N. boat.

"Damn Kiwis are everywhere these days. What island you from?" Link asked.

"North Island, near Auckland. What part of Oz you from?"

"North Queensland."

"Beautiful area. Right on the reef there? Or are you inland?"

"Right on the beach."

"Nice."

The New Zealander sat back and slid his arm around the girl.

"Nina furaha tele," the girl said as she leaned into him.

"Me, too, babe," he answered.

She and the guy beamed at each other.

"Is that some of the Maori language?" Ryan asked.

"Sorry, that was rude. My name's Kristen, Kris for short. You'll have to forgive Simon and me. We haven't seen each other in a year and half."

"Very long year and half," Simon added, and pulled her closer.

"So you've developed a secret language? And what's a Maori?" Jeanette asked while rolling her eyes.

"The Maori are the indigenous people from New Zealand, but that was actually Swahili. *Nina furaha tele* just means 'I'm really happy.' We used that a lot last year," Kristen said.

Simon smiled and nodded. "We met on a semester abroad to Kenya, fall before last. We're both into animal protection and rights. Kris is going into environmental law, and I'm deciding between marine biology or zoology. We studied and worked with an animal refuge and reserve center in Africa," Simon explained.

"Cool," Ryan said.

"I'm Marina, and this is my roommate Jeanette. Link you've already met, and this is his roommate, Ryan, from Canada."

"The fifty-first state," Jeanette chirped.

Ryan glared.

"Oh, Marina! You're the girl who was sick last night. Are you feeling better? We had lots of intestinal problems of that sort in Africa—at least here you have normal toilets," Kris said.

Marina's face flamed.

"Sick? What? When were you sick?" Jeanette looked confused.

"That's what that French girl said. What was her name?"

"That would be Rhee," Marina answered. "She seems to have taken an instant hatred to me. I have no idea why."

"Probably didn't help that she asked me out right after we arrived," Link said.

"What does that have to do with me?" Marina asked.

"Well, I might have told her I was already taking you out to dinner. She didn't seem to like that too much."

Marina's jaw dropped.

"You two went out last night?" Jeanette asked.

"No! And why did you tell her that?" Marina turned to Link.

"Well, at the time, I sort of assumed you would go if I asked. Besides, it's fun to get a rise out of girls like that. They think they're irresistible. Fun to shake them up a bit."

"Sure, at my expense."

"Aw, come on, Barbie. You would have enjoyed the look on her face. I bet it was the first time a guy turned her down. She was cool about it in front of me, like it didn't bother her. But she cursed up a storm when she went around the corner. Not in English, but it was unmistakable."

"Did you have to pardon her French?" Marina said.

They all groaned. But it was a friendly groan. Link definitely brought out the bad puns in her. She was still annoyed, but he was right. She would have loved to have seen Rhee's face. It wasn't worth the target she was sure was now on her back, but it was cool that gorgeous mean girls didn't always get their way. And, technically speaking, she sort of did have dinner with Link last night.

Chapter Four

Marco began the orientation by using a wooden mallet to bong the empty dive tank hanging outside the dining room. He walked in and jotted down their names on a seating chart on his clipboard.

"Great. If you wouldn't mind sitting at these same places each time we meet, it will make it easier for me to spot who's not here."

He took a deep breath and smiled at them. Marina could hear an audible sigh from several of the female students. Apparently, she and Jeanette weren't the only ones to notice Marco's charm.

"Welcome to the *Tiburon*. As you may remember from your orientation packet, we will be making stops in Nassau, Bahamas, in Utila in the Bay Islands of Honduras, and in Samana in the Dominican Republic. You are about to embark on your futures as adults, so on this boat you will be treated as such. This means we expect responsible behavior befitting an adult. I know many of you come from places where there is no drinking age. Let's cover that first. This boat will abide by U.S. regulations both for insurance purposes and because learning is our main goal. It doesn't matter if you are legal at home. Congratulations, you just became underage."

Amid the groans and whispers there was another stir. Rhee, dressed in all white, and Tali, in all black, were making their fashionably late arrival down in the lounge, and drawing everyone's full attention. This was largely unnecessary as they were wearing wide-brim sun hats, just one of which could have covered more than their two tiny nearly matching sundresses put together.

Jeanette snorted at the sight of them. Link chuckled with her, but Marina noticed him checking out the girls as they sashayed by. Jeanette noticed, too, and her eyes narrowed as she mouthed "Rhee?" to Marina. Marina nodded.

"They brought their own sombreros," Ryan commented.

Marina decided she really liked Ryan.

"Thank you for joining us, ladies. This brings me to

another important point. Respect. Respect for your cabin-mates, in part by not wasting their time or mine by showing up late for meetings and appointments."

Marco paused for the expected apology, an apology that did not come as the two girls were busy scoping out the room and ignoring him. Tali glanced up and saw Marco looking at the pair of them. She beamed and gave him a clueless wave. Marco shook his head in irritation. He turned back to the group.

"Respect also needs to be shown, as well as tolerance and acceptance, when we are visiting other countries and islands. We are the visitors; it is not their job to conform to what we think they should be like. It is our job to learn about their culture and avoid insulting them. You are ambassadors of your home countries, unofficial ones, but these people will be judging what they think of where you are from based on your behavior. We should do our respective countries proud and show our best side—in our language, in our actions, even in our dress. Some fashion choices might be perfectly acceptable in a place such as South Beach, but they would horrify those in the more religiously influenced communities."

Marco again looked to the two girls, who were now comparing their red nail polish. "Any questions?" he asked.

Jeanette raised her hand.

"Yes, Jeanette?"

"While we are on the subject of fashion, I just wanted to commend, um, Rhee, is it? And her little friend there, too. For their generosity in fashion choices."

Tali preened while Rhee cast a confused but suspicious glare on Jeanette, who met it with wide-eyed innocence.

"Generosity in fashion? What is this 'generosity in fashion'?" asked Rhee.

"You know, just that it is really important to protect yourself from the sun out here, and wearing a hat at all times is a great way to do so. And this way, even if someone else forgets, they can just sit in a chair close to you two and still be covered. It was just a very considerate thing to wear."

Tali sat up taller and flipped her hair back before smiling graciously. "Thank you."

"Oh, you're very welcome." Jeanette smiled back at Tali.

There were titters around the room, and Marina noticed Marco raise his eyebrows and busy himself with shuffling through some papers on his clipboard.

Link raised his hand. Marco looked relieved.

"Yes, Link?"

"I was just wondering about the Internet?"

"Oh yes, Captain says the satellite will be activated this afternoon as we get under way. Once the boat leaves port, any of you with wireless devices can access the group account with the password "Tiburon." Those who do not

have wireless-capable devices may sign up—first come, first serve; half hour max per day if it's not for research—to use the boat computer."

Marina wondered who Link was in such a hurry to e-mail. She'd been dying to e-mail Damon yesterday and tell him about the flight and the boat. But she didn't want Marco to think her head was at home and not into her experience on board, so she decided to wait to ask him about the wireless situation.

"Okay, as you already know, I am your adviser, in academic matters as well as anything else you need. On board with us are the captain and crew who will accompany the *Tiburon* once it goes into service. They will be treating you as if you were regular paying customers."

An excited murmur went up from all who had read through the luxury *Tiburon*'s brochures.

"We are all trained for ship-related and medical emergencies, which we do not expect to experience. As I was saying, respect should be shown to the other members of the crew and to myself by following our very reasonable rules and not making us be the bad guys. Because we don't much care for having to be the bad guys. Let's all just have a good time this semester, okay?"

An impromptu cheer went up from the group.

Marco grinned as he waited for everyone to calm down. "Priority one here is to learn," he continued. "In the mornings, you will have guided study sessions led by the directors or instructors from the individual facilities we visit. These will run about an hour and will outline the required reading and essay assignments.

"Much of the learning is hands-on, and you will have a chance to experience the life of a marine biologist in the field." He paused as he began handing out blank sheets of paper. "We will have focus projects in three areas of marine biology—dolphins in the Bahamas, whale sharks in Utila, and sea turtles in the Dominican Republic. On these pieces of paper, please list the areas in the order of your preference." There was a shuffling of paper and whispering as everyone made their decisions.

"What do you think?" Simon asked Kris.

"They all sound great. But whale sharks are the most unique, don't you think?"

Marina knew exactly what she wanted. She printed out: 1. Dolphins 2. Sea Turtles 3. Whale Sharks. She looked up to compare choices with her roommate's and noticed Link scanning her list with disturbing interest. She slid her hand over the top and folded it quickly.

"Please finish up and pass your papers to me."

Marco collected the lists and looked through them. "Well, it looks like our groups will work out very easily. Please listen for your names. For the sea turtle focus project, the group will include Jeanette, Ryan, Tali, and Rhee."

Jeanette turned to Marina and rolled her eyes. "Ugh, Ryan's in my group," she whispered.

"That will be cool. He's great."

"Ryan? Puh-lease. Boooring," Jeanette whispered back. "And we have to deal with Rhee and Tali."

Marina smirked. "Poor you and Ryan!"

Jeanette laughed. "More like, poor sea turtles."

Marco continued, "For our dolphin focus project, the group will be Sam, Marina . . ."

At the sound of her name, Marina broke out into a wide grin. She was finally going to study dolphins in a real research facility—certainly much different than studying marine life in the murky waters of Lake Champlain.

"Maaike and Link. You will be studying dolphins at the research center in the Bahamas."

Wait, did he just say Link? Marina's grin slowly faded as she looked over at Link, who smiled and winked.

Marco finished listing the two whale-shark focus groups. "The reason we have these groups is that the facilities are small. While everyone will get a taste of the work performed in each port, only the focus group will interact on a daily basis with the staff. After the morning study sessions, those who have been assigned to that specific focus project will break off and perform their special research at the facility. The rest of you will have free time to explore the island and complete your assignments on your own schedule. Any questions?"

A murmur went through the group.

"In the port of your chosen focus group, I will expect a

thoroughly researched four- to six-page essay about a specific aspect of your focus animal. For the other two ports, a shorter two- to four-page essay, which encompasses your experience as a whole, will be fine. You might want to include your observations and thoughts on the people and place, besides just concentrating on the marine life. Your grade will be based on a combination of your essays, your attendance at the daily lectures led by each facility's staff, and your work in the field.

"Each segment of our trip will last about two weeks. It might seem like you'll have a lot of free time, with only a one-hour lecture each day, but you should take advantage of the other opportunities for experiencing life as a marine biologist."

Marco stopped and waited until everyone looked up from their notes.

"It's going to take some time to ready the ship for departure, so I need you all to stay on the boat this morning and come back to this room by one o'clock. Bear with us, this is just a part of life at sea."

Everyone groaned.

"I know, I know. But the good news is you can spend the morning studying!"

Marco chuckled at their distraught faces before continuing.

"Just teasing. You'll have free time to get to know one another. But you just may want to study when you hear

what the good folks at Tiburon have in store for you."

Marco ended with a dramatic pause and looked around to make sure he had their attention. Even Rhee had an expectant look on her face.

"The Tiburon fleet, which provides luxury dive trips in places as exotic as the Galápagos Islands and the Micronesian islands of Chuuk and Palau..."

Marina held her breath.

"Have generously donated a free weeklong excursion to the destination of choice for the top two students!"

This was amazing. Marina had surfed online and read up on the company when she got the news they would be using one of their boats for the semester. It cost almost a thousand dollars a day to be pampered by the crew of the Tiburon and to be led by and learn from the expertise of some of the best divers in the world. Everyone else must have known this, too, because the chattering among the students was drowning out what Marco was saying.

"We have two free trips, which include airfare, transfers, and everything else involved in the usual Tiburon setup, for our top two students. To motivate you to work beyond the scope of your individual research interests, we have set up a bonus points system. These 'TripTasks' will be in the form of hands-on facility experiences that offer practical knowledge. Let me emphasize, these TripTasks are voluntary extra credit."

Marco checked to make sure they were all following

him. Marina could feel her attraction to him slip away as he talked. He was friendly, but very much in teacher mode. It made him seem a lot older than he first had at the airport. So much for a distracting harmless crush to keep her mind off missing Damon.

She didn't realize she'd glazed over until Link's pen scratched out "Earth to Barbie—Thinking of me?" on his notebook. Marina's faced flamed as she shot Link a look. Well, at least she had a distraction of some sort. "Harmless" didn't seem the right word for it though. She ignored him and tuned back into Marco.

"At the end of the semester, the two students with the top academic scores overall will win the incentive. You'll have a year to use your prize."

There was cheering and howling, and Marco waited with a smile for them to quiet down.

"Okay, okay. Here's a folder of brochures from the Tiburon fleet. Take this morning to relax. But remember to be back here by one o'clock. We expect to pull out of the dock around two."

Marco disappeared into the kitchen as the students pounced on the folder. Simon brought back a big handful of brochures and plopped them in the middle of the table. Marina sat up and flipped through them with the others until she came upon the Galápagos brochure. The remote island where Darwin's evolution played out had intrigued her for years. She had even bought the DVD

of the Discovery special highlighting the islands—largely untouched by man—and all of the amazing creatures that inhabited it.

She tried to slide the brochure out from the pile and realized someone else was tugging on it as well. She looked up and met Link's eyes. Her heart skipped a beat.

"Go ahead, Barbie. Ladies first."

The morning crawled by as they waited to depart. Marina took Marco's advice and read the first few chapters of her *Introduction to Marine Biology* textbook. A lot of it was review, since she was an avid Discovery Channel viewer whenever anything sea-related came on. And she usually surfed the Net after the shows for more information on the different creatures featured. Now that she was here, she couldn't wait to see it all for herself.

When she entered the lounge that afternoon, Marina saw that everyone, just as Marco had requested, had gravitated back to the same spots. Link wasted no time continuing his flirtation with Jeanette. He sat in the booth with one arm draped casually over Jeanette's freckled shoulder. It was hard to tell if Jeanette was into him, but she didn't seem to mind the attention. Link patted the seat on the other side of him when he saw Marina come in.

"How was your morning? Didn't see you much in the lounge. Not seasick, were you?"

"Nope, just chilled out and enjoyed the view."

It was amazing how quick the sexist overkill toward Marina had dropped. Even his tone of voice was different when he spoke to her now. He was actually being a nice guy.

Marco came in and counted the students. He checked his seating chart and walked over to Rhee.

"Where's your cabinmate?"

"In the toilet. *Vomiting*." Rhee sniffed. "She is not much of a boater for someone who grew up in the bayouuuu." Rhee drawled out the word "bayou" attempting a thick southern accent while rolling her eyes.

"Nice friend," Ryan said under his breath.

"Good thing she's so hot," Link agreed.

Jeanette stiffened and slid out from under Link's arm. She bent to tie her sandals. Marina noticed Jeanette's sandals were actually thongs and gave her a sympathetic smile when she came back up. Jeanette half smiled back and shrugged her shoulders. She feigned interest in Ryan's fish book and scooted out of Link's reach. So that was that for Link and Jeanette. Link just was what he was. Marina was grateful to have a reminder of why she didn't want to be the one in his sights.

"Well, I'll just go on, and you can fill in Tali later," Marco said.

Rhee nodded with a dramatic sigh and went back to wearing her ultra-bored look.

With a smile, Marco turned to everyone and said, "So,

does anyone here feel like going to the Bahamas?"

They all laughed. The big boat rumbled as the engines started.

"Say good-bye to the United States; we are on our way!"

Cheers went up as everyone craned to get a glimpse of the docks as the crew released the boat. Marco took notice and smiled.

"Go on then, people. Why don't you head to the outer deck and give a proper bon voyage. Then meet back here in three hours for dinner—in the Bahamas!"

Their excited laughter echoed off the cabin walls. Marina jumped up to head outside with the others. Her huge smile was hurting her cheeks.

Marina and Jeanette waved a last good-bye to Coconut Grove as the boat slid past the other yachts and headed out to the channel. Hitting the ocean, it gave a lurch left then right as it adjusted to the angle of the swells. As the boat turned and started its course west, it settled into a slow rhythmic sway.

"One hand for the boat, one hand for yourselves at all times, guys. Rails are there for a reason!" Marco's voice called above the whoosh of the wind, "If you are feeling ill effects from the motion, please come see me. Don't just hide away in your cabin—that won't help. Best to stay above with the fresh air and stare at a fixed point or the line of the horizon once we are out of sight of the land."

"We are going to be out of sight of land? That is so cool!" Jeanette said as she leaned against the rail.

Marina's skin tingled. The fresh sea breeze and occasional salty spray refreshed her sun-tightened face. The combination dulled everything else, and she hugged onto the rail next to Jeanette as the boat swayed.

It was utter contentment. She looked across the group and saw Simon and Kristen. Simon was behind Kristen, resting his chin on her shoulder. A little twinge hit Marina's chest. Damon liked to do that. She was dying to e-mail him. She tried to push it away and get back the contented sensation of the moment before. But it was too late, the magic had slipped away. Missing Damon took over. This was the longest they had been out of touch since they'd met.

This was the sort of back and forth pull she worried would follow her if she went to U of H. Wanting to be in the moment, living her new life, but pulled out of it to check up on things at home. It wasn't a good sign that they had barely left and she was already fighting it.

"Meet you back at the cabin," Marina told Jeanette finally.

From: Marinabiology@email.com
To: SkierBoi@email.com
Subject: Miss you sooooooo much!

Hey, Da! I was hoping you might be online so we could IM. You wouldn't believe this boat! It's just like the brochure I showed you. We don't see the crew much, but Marco, he's our counselor for everything, said they were ironing all the kinks out of running a brand-new boat. My roommate, Jeanette, seems really cool. She's from the Midwest. There are students here from about every country you could think of.

Sorry I didn't e-mail when we got here, we just got connected this morning. There was this amazing sunset last night, so much more colorful and real somehow than the ones back home. Btw, was your connection screwed up again? I didn't see any messages waiting when I signed on.

Anyway, wish you were here! Love you!

M.

Jeanette walked in as Marina was signing off.

"Ooooh! You have a laptop?"

"Yes, present from my parents. They were really excited for me about coming."

Jeanette kicked off her flip-flops and used the edge of Marina's bunk to launch herself onto her bed.

"Can I borrow it? I'd sign up downstairs, but it's already booked until this afternoon."

"Sure. E-mailing a boyfriend?"

Jeanette snorted.

"Hardly. My dad."

Marina rolled over and looked up at Jeanette's bunk.

"He gets worried. I can't wait for this summer. I get some space to breathe when I'm at my mom's place in Detroit. It was a big thing for Dad even to let me come here. Good thing, though. I would have gone mental at home in St. Louis for another six weeks."

"Why, what's at home?"

"Nothing. Just my dad. All the time, every single minute of my life. You know how dads are."

Marina picked at the hem of her T-shirt and thought about that for a minute.

"I hardly see mine actually."

"Your parents divorced, too?"

"No, my dad's just pretty busy with his development deals."

"Development deals?"

"His work, along with local politics. I don't even know what he does really. But he has a cell phone permanently attached to one ear, with a second phone available should the first happen to fail him. And when they're not ringing, his BlackBerry's going off. He's very noisy for someone who doesn't talk much."

"Weird."

"I guess. Mom's usually tucked away in her office or showing houses. We all do our own thing."

Marina rolled back over and idly surfed the Net.

"I wish I could have a life like that. I mean, it would be nice to have my own laptop. My dad's afraid I'll run into someone evil in the big, bad cyberworld. So we have Internet in the living room, where he can monitor me. He's big into monitoring."

"I never would have guessed."

Marina blushed when Jeanette laughed, then said, "I didn't mean that in a bad way, just—"

"No, it's okay. I know what you mean. Anyway, would you mind if I put in my daily contact with him? I can get it out of the way and not have to worry about it later."

"Oh, sure."

Marina closed her IM and e-mail windows and handed her laptop up.

"Hey! Who's the hottie?"

Marina flushed. She'd forgotten about her laptop wallpaper. It was a shot of Damon and her at the top of Mount Mansfield a few months after they'd met. She stood up next to Jeanette's bunk and looked at the screen for a second. Damon had one arm around her, and they were laughing into the camera. Seeing it always made her happy and sad at once. They looked like two entirely different people than they were now. She missed that couple. She shook her head and smiled at Jeanette. She didn't want to get into that with a perfect stranger.

"Just a friend from home," Marina fibbed.

"Well, he's cute."

"Yeah."

Marina laid back down in her bunk and spun Dude around by his side pectoral fins, listening to Jeanette tap away to her dad.

Chapter Five

The tiny islands of the Bahamas looked like pictures on postcards, like something you never really expected to see in person. The pale beaches glowed next to aqua water so clear you could see through it to check out the fish swimming below. On the shoreline were masses of palms, and the beach was dotted with little tiki huts in bright colors. Marina leaned onto the rail and watched all the passing tourists play in the surf. There were a few windsurfers in the distance, and every few hundred yards there were big signs advertising parasailing and snorkeling trips. Jeanette joined her at the rail and pointed to a small speedboat taking off with a bikini-clad girl harnessed into a parasail on the back.

"I am all over that! Hope we have time," she said.

Ryan walked past behind them and looked up from his fish-identification book to watch the parasailer. The bright red-and-yellow parachute filled with air and started whipping around behind the boat.

"Death trap, those," he said.

Jeanette gave him a withering look.

"You only live once, you know," she said.

"Yeah, so why not make it last," Ryan reasoned, heading down toward the lounge for dinner.

"It's about *how* you live your life," Jeanette muttered.

Marina smiled. Those two were like oil and water.

Marina woke the next morning, refreshed and more rested than she ever remembered being. Some of the other students had stayed up after dinner, hanging out on deck and watching the nightlife on the shoreline. But marine biology was her dream career, and she was not going to let socializing make her too tired to enjoy what might be her first interaction with dolphins. She was worried the excitement would keep her up, but the sway of the boat had rocked her into a deep sleep.

Jeanette breezed in with coffee again, already dressed

in a midriff-baring sarong outfit similar to the one she'd worn the day before. Marina could see the strings of her bikini sticking out around her neck.

"Morning, Sunshine!"

"Thanks, this is really sweet of you," Marina said, taking the coffee.

"No prob. I figured I'd sneak in some bonus points early since I'm sure I'll do something to annoy you sooner or later."

Marina laughed and sipped the warm liquid. "I doubt it," she said, "I'm pretty laid back."

"Well, I know I can be a little much for some people. But I like the way I am. So I just pump up the thoughtfulness to balance it out."

Marina's laugh ended in a snort.

"Oh my *God*! Did you just snort?"

Marina blushed.

"That is the cutest thing ever!" Jeanette said.

"Yeah, right."

"No, seriously. It's a good thing, you know. Makes it easier for me not to hate you for the way you look." She winked. "Meet you downstairs!"

Marina walked over to the mirror and shook her head at her reflection. Hate her for the way she looked? She just didn't see it. Only everyday plain-Jane Marina stared back at her. She sighed and went to sift through her bag for a swimsuit. She pulled out her red Speedo, black surf shorts, and Damon's BOARD TILL YOU DROP! T-shirt.

She was missing him this morning. She'd checked her messages last night before bed and again when she woke up, but he'd never e-mailed back. Probably out with the ski team all night. In the past year, Damon had spent more and more time with the team, practicing and at meets, and hanging out after. Before he got caught up with it, he and Marina had spent most of their free time together. Now he seemed only to look forward to the next ski competition.

He claimed the ski team was just a good way to deal with the stress of his mom's illness, but it became so much more than that when he admitted he didn't want to go to the University of Hawaii anymore. He wanted stay in Vermont—close to the slopes, and close to family. And he wanted her to stay with him. But community college in Vermont wasn't exactly what she'd worked so hard for these past three years.

The bonging of the dive tank startled her. She grabbed her marine bio book and ran down to the dining area.

She was one of the last in and slid into the booth next to Kristen. Jeanette had snagged her a plate full of eggs and bacon and slid it over to her with a smile. Marina was starving and dove in while she listened to Marco.

"So, good news, guys! I already met with Immigration, and they are pretty lax in this port compared to some of the others we'll be encountering. Comes from the high tourist load and the many day-trippers in their speedboats who pop over from Miami. Your passports have been stamped, and they've gone back into the captain's possession for safekeeping."

Marina was kind of bummed. She'd never been out of the country except for drives up to Montreal and had sort of been looking forward to using her passport for the first time.

"So, run back up to your cabins and grab your books. Domenico, a dolphin trainer and marine biologist from the Bahamian Marine Research Institute, will be here in twenty minutes for your first lecture. After that, there will be a bus outside waiting to take those of you in the dolphin focus group to the facility. The rest of you are free to explore the island. Sign out in groups of two or more, please. Within two hours, you could be dipping your toes for the first time into the Caribbean Sea!"

Chapter Six

Marina flipped through her book and reread the same intro page on dolphins for the fifth time. They were all sitting back at their tables waiting on the arrival of their first instructor. Her heart thudded as the tall, lanky guy walked into the dining area. This was going to be her mentor in the world of dolphins, and she worried she'd do something stupid. He was laughing with Marco about something, and Marina relaxed as soon as she saw the guy's wide smile. He looked young like Marco, probably in his early twenties. His blue T-shirt had a logo for the Bahamian Marine

Research Institute on the back, and ANIMAL CARE STAFF was written above the chest pocket.

"Everyone, please welcome Domenico to the boat," Marco said. "He'll be your instructor here at the facility for the next two weeks. As I said before, he'll be running the lecture sessions, and those of you working on the dolphin focus project will be working closely with him during our stay."

"Hello everyone, and welcome to Nassau," Domenico started good-naturedly. "I've spent my life right here on the island, with the exception of four years at the University of Miami, where I studied marine biology, with a concentration on marine mammals. I hope you have a great time and get to enjoy my home and all it has to offer. I'll try not to load you down with too much homework or papers so you get a chance to explore the islands."

There was a collective murmur of relief.

"First, an introduction to the islands. Anyone know what happened in 1492? That year ring any bells?"

"Columbus discovered America?" someone in back offered.

"Close. Columbus discovered the Bahamas! He landed on a small island called San Salvador and, noting the shallow water, named the area 'baja mar.' Anyone speak Spanish? Please, tell us what 'baja mar' means?"

Marina raised her hand. "Low sea?"

"Very good. 'Baja mar,' Bahama, the Bahamas, Islands

of the Shallow Sea. Fought over in history, eventually being granted our freedom from Great Britain in 1964, we became our very own nation on July 10, 1973. Okay, history lesson over. The current population is three hundred thousand, living on—anyone want to guess how many islands?"

"Twenty?" Kristen tried.

"Ten?" said Teresa.

"Seven!" yelled a somewhat green-faced Tali.

"That's right. Seven"—he paused—"hundred! Seven hundred islands here in the Bahamas. In case you were wondering, sorry, but no, you will not be visiting all of them."

Scattered laughter broke out.

"You are now in the capital of the Bahamas. Our sister island, Paradise Island, is right across the way. Those of you not in the focus research group should find plenty to do during your stay."

Marina absently doodled a jumping dolphin in the margin of her manual.

"Now more about our facility. We have twenty-one Atlantic bottlenose dolphins. Seven were born in captivity, six were collected from wild pods, and the rest came from facilities that could no longer afford to give them a proper home. You might wonder why an institute dedicated to marine research would offer something so commercial as our dolphin show programs. Obviously, the proper medical care and feed for the dolphins costs a great deal of money. The dolphin swims, behavior demonstrations, and dives we offer with the animals cover the cost of their care."

Several of the students were scribbling notes. Domenico paused and waited for them to look up before continuing.

"But a far more important reason for exposing these particular dolphins to the public is education. We have found that making a personal connection with the natural beauty of marine life does more to change lifelong bad habits than years of lectures and advertisements. If you touch a dolphin, watch their behavior, see their intelligence—you will not only go on to behave in an ecologically friendly way, but to tell others of your experience and prompt a change in their behavior as well. In this way, we hope to affect greater change to protect the ocean habitat and those animals that make it their home."

It was inspiring to see the trainer's passion for the animals.

"So that is our philosophy. I will be teaching you more about the animals in our morning sessions."

Domenico paused for a moment to let them catch up on their notes.

"If you aren't in my focus group, you may also take part, on a space-available basis, in the swims and dives where we observe dolphin behavior. You were all required to be certified scuba divers in order to be in this program, so you are all set to participate."

A wave of excitement went through the room. This would be a very popular option and hard to get a spot. Marina was glad that by being in the dolphin focus group, she was guaranteed a chance to work up-close with the animals.

"In addition, three times a day, you may accompany the trainers as they feed the dolphins. This is strictly a hands-off time, since the trainers use this time to enhance their bond with their dolphin. But they do work with the animals on learning behaviors, as well as check them out to make sure they are healthy and happy. So there will be a lot to see and learn. It will be an excellent opportunity to ask questions either about the dolphins or about what a trainer's life is really like. Several trainers have come here from bigger, more commercial centers in the United States. You can talk with them about the contrast between facility philosophies."

Marina wondered if she and Link and Maaike and Sam would be doing the feeding or if the hands-off rule applied to the focus group as well.

"I've been considering possible options for your TripTask program. Off the top of my head, I know that our research department could use help with inputting data from a recent wild dolphin population trip. It's mostly clerical work, but that could be a good opportunity. As I think of other appropriate tasks, I will announce them during our morning lectures."

Domenico looked around.

"Now, in case I have completely turned you off, there are some things that make all the data inputting worthwhile. One of those is the birth of a new animal. When I said we had twenty-one dolphins, I wasn't being entirely accurate. We actually have twenty-one and a half. Gracie, one of our mature female dolphins, is pregnant. She is due to have her baby any day now, and you just might be lucky enough for it to happen while you are here. A baby dolphin is a huge draw for tourists, but it is even more personal for us trainers since the animals we are paired with are like our family."

Marina tried to contain her excitement. Seeing a brand-new baby dolphin would be the highlight of a lifetime!

"Judging by all your smiling faces, I can see you understand how important this is! Now, I am letting you off early for your first day. Your assignment is to go and get acquainted with my island. There is a bus waiting outside for those in the focus study group. We'll head out for the facility in fifteen minutes. Please grab your bags and meet me outside."

Chapter Seven

"Welcome to the Bahamian Marine Research Institute," Domenico said to Marina, Maaike, Sam, and Link. "I thought I'd start you out with the fun part of the job, and let you meet some of the dolphins. You will be observing me train today, but by the end of your stay, you will learn several hand signals for behavior and will have the opportunity to try them out. For now, I will take you through a typical behavior demonstration we might do for tourists preparing for a dolphin swim. The actual dolphin show, which we perform for a much larger group, is more involved."

A whoosh from the water made Marina jump as the dolphins came up for air. She fought to keep focused on Domenico.

"These wide wooden bleachers that frame the dolphins' swimming area are for tourists to sit and watch demonstrations. In front of the bleachers we have a long rectangle enclosure. As you can see, the walls are made of net with four-inch-square holes so that the ocean tides as well as small plants and sea life can pass through. The top of the net walls are hung under the wooden boardwalks that allow us to walk around the enclosure and interact with our dolphins. The bottom of these nets are anchored deep under the sandy floor of the sea. No concrete pools or tanks here."

Domenico spoke with pride, and Marina could see why. It looked like as natural an environment as was possible for a captive dolphin.

"This enclosure is twenty to thirty feet deep and extends right out from the shoreline facility, where we have a small museum and our labs. The shedlike building at the end of the bleachers is actually a state-of-the-art fish house, where all the dolphins' food is prepared."

Marina could see a dozen other trainers walking along the boardwalks of a larger enclosure, the size of a football field. Some were walking into the waist-high water straight from the little beach, and others stood on top of the boardwalks. She could see them giving hand signals, and occasionally a bottlenose dolphin would jump from the sea.

Domenico led them around the narrow boardwalk of the facility to the far side, facing the bleachers. Marina was dying to check out the dolphins, but she tried to ignore the spouting of the animals in the water so she wouldn't trip and fall in.

A six-foot-by-eight-foot platform made out of sturdy blue foam was anchored to the boardwalk and floated on top of the water facing the deserted stands. Domenico stepped down onto the platform, which bobbed slightly under his weight. He reached up and gave Marina a hand. She wobbled as she stepped down on the platform.

"Go ahead and have a seat, right on the edge there. Just dangle your legs in the water. The dolphins might get curious and come check you out."

Maaike, a student from Holland, sat down next to her. Domenico sat in the middle, leaving Sam and Link to find space on the other side. Domenico smiled around a thin stick-shaped whistle held between his teeth, and checked that they were all settled in.

He raised his hands as if he was going to lead an orchestra. A trio of Atlantic bottlenose dolphins popped up in front of him. He gave a sharp trill of the whistle. Marina and the group oohed and ahhed. It was hard not to be impressed. These were the show dolphins that performed for large groups of tourists and locals. Marina thought the education angle and meeting the dolphins was an effective method for promoting ecological awareness. She had spent only seconds in the dolphins' presence, and already she couldn't imagine anyone being so heartless as to litter. She knew that rain would eventually wash litter debris out to sea, and could endanger the lives of dolphins and other sea creatures.

Domenico pulled out a cooler. When he opened the cover, it revealed a mound of ice. He held his hands up again, and all three dolphins seemed to perk up. Their heads rose a bit higher above the water, and their eyes were locked on Domenico's hands. With a whooshing movement, he threw one arm high above his head, and they dove down in unison.

Marina looked at the water and back at the trainer's raised arm. She caught something out of the corner of her eye and looked back to see all three dolphins launching themselves high out of the water in perfect arcs. They disappeared again, and, with a little flick of his hand on the still raised arm, they jumped again and then a third time. As they rose to their highest point on the third jump, the whistle trilled and Domenico rummaged through the cooler. The dolphins popped up in front of the float, and he tossed them each a fish with one hand. Maaike and Marina clapped in delight.

"So, who would like to take a turn?" Domenico asked.

Marina shifted uncomfortably.

"Marina, how about you?" The trainer's white teeth flashed on the side of his thin black whistle. "Come on, give it a try." He handed Marina the whistle.

"Me? No. I mean, I don't know what I'm doing," Marina stammered.

"It's okay. You won't hurt them. And they know it. They have an instinct for people. It may seem like they are just doing what we ask to earn a fish, but the bond between trainer and dolphin is what makes them want to do what they are asked. We use a version of Skinner's operant conditioning. Never any negative consequences, only positive reinforcement. They like the praise, enjoy the attention. We just ignore any negative behavior."

Marina paused for a minute. She took a deep breath and raised her arms conductor-like. To her surprise, the dolphins seemed to perk up. She glanced sideways and saw Link leaning so far forward on the platform he was almost falling in. He was smiling.

She sat up straighter to focus and made eye contact with the dolphins. It might have been her imagination, but their eyes seemed to widen with anticipation. She whooshed her right arm down and then flicked it high over her head the way Domenico had. They paused for a millisecond and then hopped up and dove backward into the sea. Marina sat with her arm raised for what felt like an eternity. Maybe they weren't going to jump; maybe they'd just ditched her. She gasped as they came out of the sea, dripping great arcs of water off their muscular bodies. As they dropped down, barely making a ripple, she glanced again to the left. Domenico was nodding with a smile, and Link was grinning.

Almost too late she remembered the little hand flick as they came out again. It seemed to egg them on to jump higher. They dropped down again, and Marina giggled in excitement. Domenico grabbed his whistle, and when they reappeared the last time, he expertly gave a sharp blast and clapped for a blushing Marina. Domenico pushed the cooler of fish toward her.

"Careful of the fins, and toss them headfirst," he instructed.

Marina wouldn't have dared feed them on her own ten minutes ago, but she felt such a rush at that moment she thought she could do anything. She plunged her hand into the melting ice and pulled out three fish, each a bit smaller than her hand. Using both hands she tried to toss them headfirst. The first two went well, although she almost smacked the first dolphin in the face. The dolphin darted back and snapped the fish down in one gulp. The third flew from her hands and flipped en route, landing in the dolphin's mouth tail first. She paled, scared it would swallow it and damage its throat with the spiky fins, but the dolphin spit it out, neatly spinning the treat around, and swallowed it headfirst without a problem. It laid back on its side looking at her for a moment before swimming up and sliding its noselike rostrum onto her leg.

"He likes you," Link called.

Marina laughed and petted the dolphin's rubbery skin, being careful to avoid the delicate blowhole. She really felt like pinching herself. She laughed in delight at the dolphin's antics as it pulled back and snapped its jaws shut to spit water onto her leg.

Domenico gathered the dolphins back with the attention hand signal, and they were all business again. With a flick of his hands sideways while pointing with his index fingers he casually sent the dolphins flying around the enclosure on a speed swim.

"They are reaching speeds of twenty miles an hour. They don't sustain this for long swims, but often use this sort of speed in short bursts when hunting in the wild. Occasionally, when a school of their favorite food, goggle-eyes, pass through the net walls, we can see them doing that inside the enclosure," Domenico said.

A great rooster tail of water splashed over their legs as the dolphins skidded back in and stopped right at their feet. It reminded Marina of the way she'd slide to a stop skiing or ice-skating. She thought briefly of Damon, who was probably doing that very thing thousands of miles north.

She let the beauty of the animals sway her attention as

Domenico taught the students the hand signals for flip, twist, chatter, and finally even walk backward, as they propelled their entire body's weight above the sea using their muscular flukes or tails.

They broke for lunch at the facility's outdoor café, where Marina's group of four joined the rest of the trainers in a local meal of fish tacos. The tables were set up on a deck overlooking the enclosure where they had spent the morning.

The locals loaded their plates with tacos and drizzled some homemade hot sauce on top. Domenico looked up and passed Marina the jar of hot sauce with a smile. She put about four drops of the stuff onto her taco. She bit into the flaky flour tortilla, and a medley of sweet fish mixed with the tangy pepper strips and spicy vinegar hot sauce filled her mouth. Her eyes widened in delight.

As they ate, Marina noticed that tourists and a few locals with their children were filing into the wooden bench stands for the show. Link got up to grab a third taco from the platter. When Domenico scooted back and walked away from the table, Link slid into the trainer's empty chair and sat next to Marina. Maaike and Sam seemed pretty cozy at the next table down.

"You did great down there," Link said. "The dolphins really followed what you asked. That must have been cool."

Marina smiled at the memory. "It was a rush. Like going

over the big hill on a roller coaster—times a thousand."

"I know what you mean. I felt that same way the first time I guided a raft on my own. I can't wait to try my hand at this," he said.

Marina nodded, happy that Link understood.

The tourists were pointing at the group of trainers and taking pictures like they were celebrities. Marina sat straighter. Most of the trainers seemed used to the attention, but a few of the younger teenagers posed and played up for the cameras. A warm feeling spread through her, and it took a moment for her to recognize it as pride. That feeling only grew warmer as Domenico returned and tossed matching blue T-shirts on the table next to their plates.

"If you're going to sit with the trainers, you'd better look like the trainers. You guys are done for the day. The bus will take you back when you're ready. Go ahead and wear those while you're here at the institute. I'll see you all in the morning. Maybe after the study session, we'll go out to the key and see the rest of the dolphins. We might even catch a glimpse of one very pregnant dolphin," Domenico said.

Marina yanked off Damon's oversize shirt and pulled the blue one over her suit. She smiled at the word STAFF printed over the pocket.

"Looks great on you," Link said. His blue eyes sparkled, and Marina knew he really meant it.

She waffled between wanting to dissuade any hint of

flirting and enjoying the moment of sharing the incredible experience. Link got it. Damon, well, it was nothing personal, he just didn't care much about marine biology.

She'd reconnect with Da tonight. He probably hadn't sent her any e-mails on purpose. She knew he acted angry when he was hurt. It was just his way of dealing. And her leaving town for two months had definitely hurt him. After three years, she understood his ways, even if she didn't always like them. In the meantime, it couldn't hurt to be polite to Link.

"Thanks," she said at last.

Link stood and peeled off his shirt. Marina averted her eyes to stop herself from counting his abs. Maybe it *could* hurt to be polite to Link. She exhaled and stepped away from the table as he pulled on the facility shirt.

"I'm gonna go talk to Maaike for a bit," she said.

"Oh, okay. What are you doing this afternoon?"

Marina considered telling him she'd be trying to reach her boyfriend, but there didn't seem to be any point. She had already set up the "friends only" ground rules with Link. She just needed to keep her distance.

"I'm not sure; I have a few things to do. I want to start researching topics for my paper," she said.

Link nodded as Marina walked away.

She sat down by Sam and Maaike at the trainers' table. Most of the workers seemed younger than she was. She always assumed that to be a dolphin trainer it would take years and years of college and then scrubbing tank walls for another decade in some aquarium while waiting for the chance to work with the animals. This sure wasn't the States. And the facility sure wasn't like the Sea World she remembered, either. Everything down here just seemed more laid back, more natural, sort of a tropical version of Vermont. It felt like home.

Chapter Eight

Marina spent the afternoon checking her e-mail every 3.4 seconds. Or at least it felt that way. She started out sending a cheerful, "Hey, what's up, did you get my message?" e-mail to Damon. Four hours and six e-mails later she was feeling like an idiot since she was sure her light and breezy "miss you" messages had turned into totally needy and whiny "I miss you. Is everything okay? Please come on IM or e-mail to let me know you're not mad!" notes.

It was as if the distance had made her feel like a stranger. Each hour that passed made her second- and third-guess what he might be thinking. Damon wasn't much of a talker, and without being there—close enough to be able to read his body language—she couldn't stop her growing uncertainty.

She finally had to remind herself that this was just Damon. Her Damon. After three years together, she was perfectly entitled to send him twenty messages, whiny or not, from this far away. Then she felt better. It was Saturday afternoon. So he was probably just skiing or boarding.

She liked to say that she had a renaissance man, since most guys did one or the other. Damon said it gave him different vibes. He snowboarded with his buddies for fun, and then had no problem slipping into competition-style skiing with the team. Everyone was impressed with it. She used to be, too, but it took up so much of his time.

And now obsessing over this was taking too much of her time. She'd wasted her first afternoon in the Bahamas on a dumb laptop. She checked IM one last time, but the little offline smiley was fast asleep. She considered screaming at it to see if it would wake up. Yep, she was a goner. Cabin fever had taken over.

She grabbed a book and dragged herself out of her bunk. Most of the students were on day trips around the island, but she could at least chill out on one of the chaises. Maybe get a bit of a base tan. At least she knew Damon'd be online after dinner. They had a standing Saturday-night IM date. She'd live until then.

• • •

Teresa stood next to Marina in the line for drinks.

"You're in this focus group, aren't you?" Teresa asked.

"Yep," said Marina.

"Lucky you!"

"Yep!"

They laughed together as they shuffled closer to the coolers filled with iced tea, lemonade, and water. Teresa was keeping a wary eye on Tali, who stood in line in front of her. Tali had gotten her hair braided by one of the locals on the beach. She was turning her head back and forth, spinning her tiny blonde braids, which were armored by a rainbow of beads, around in a dangerous arc. Rhee, who stood in front of Tali, turned and slammed her glass down on the counter.

"Stop that!" she demanded.

"It feels so cool, though," Tali said.

"You look like such a...a tourist," Rhee hissed.

Tali stopped, and her braids dropped down on to her shoulders.

Marina shook her head at the pair and smiled at Teresa.

"So, what did you do today?" Marina asked.

"I haven't been diving in a long time. I studied up on that, mostly. Those diving physics figures are killing me. I can never remember the right formulas."

"I know. It's my one worry with majoring in marine biology. All the science and math will be a challenge."

They stepped forward as Tali finished pouring a glass of half tea/half lemonade.

"I can help you with your math if you want," Tali said to Teresa.

Teresa looked at the girl as Tali started swinging her braids again. She began to stammer a "No, thanks," but Marina grabbed her arm to stop her.

"That's right! Tali's amazing with numbers," Marina said.

Teresa gave her a dubious look.

"Really," Marina whispered.

"Well, thanks then, Tali. That'd be great. Maybe after dinner?" Teresa called over her shoulder as she headed to her usual table.

"Sure!" said Tali.

"Let's go, Tali!" Rhee yelled imaptiently.

Marina shook her head and slid into the booth next to Jeanette. It was a shame Tali wasn't as good at choosing friends as she was at doing math.

"What did you guys do this afternoon?" Marina asked Kristen and Simon.

"We had the best day!" said Simon. "We went to this place called The Retreat. It has the largest collection of rare palms anywhere, and the place is just sitting there in the middle of a residential neighborhood. It's the headquarters for the Bahamas National Trust, which is in charge of all the National Parks on the islands."

"They're looking for volunteers to help in the gardens. We're thinking of asking Marco if that might qualify for extra credit, since we'd be learning about ecology."

"Sounds cool," said Jeanette.

"Very cool!" Marina agreed. But not nearly as cool as getting three dolphins to jump for you, she thought.

"There were all these rare palms and orchids growing everywhere, and a little stream, too. It was so shadowy green and peaceful," Kristen said.

"Reminded me of the Botanical Gardens back home in Auckland, only more tropical."

"That sounds like a good place for photos," Ryan said. "I'm glad I brought my camera. I almost didn't since they have the newest gear on board for underwater shots. Some of their equipment I've only read about in my photography catalogues. They don't even carry it up in Canada."

"Of course you would have photography catalogues," Jeanette smirked.

"Well, I know my professional journals can't measure up to the eloquence of *Cosmo*, or whatever, but I happen to take my future career seriously."

"Oh my *God*, you are seventeen! Get over yourself, let your hair down—if you have any under that hat you never take off."

Marina tuned out their bickering. She couldn't believe the two of them voluntarily spent the day together studying on the beach. They must be into torture. As tortured as you could get lounging on a Bahamian beach, that is.

"So should we head up and stake out the chaise lounge area for a little Welcome to the Bahamas party?" Link asked.

Everyone agreed and chatted about what music to bring up and where to get some sodas.

"Hey guys, I think I'm calling it a night," Marina said. "You go on, I'm just gonna take it easy. I don't want to be too tired to enjoy the dolphins tomorrow."

It might have been her imagination, but she thought she caught a disappointed look from Link. All the more reason to skip the party. Besides, with Jeanette gone, there was plenty of privacy for a nice long talk with Damon. Maybe they could turn things around and get back what Simon and Kristen had, and what they seemed to have lost.

Two hours and ten minutes later Marina was afraid she was imagining Damon's little messenger smiley waking up. Marina was so happy to see him, she forgot about the wait.

M: OMG OMG OMG, YAY!

D: what

M: Finally! You're here!

D: i said i would be

M: I know, I just missed you.

D: likewise

Marina took a deep breath. He was still mad. On their four-month anniversary, she was the first one to say "I love you." And he had said "Likewise." It had crushed her and they almost broke up over it. Now it was a kind of private joke at certain times, and how he let her know he was pissed at other times. She had a feeling she knew which it was this time.

M: Anyway, I can't wait to tell you, I had the best day ever!

D: really

M: We went to the dolphin thing & the guy let me try to make them do something. I did & when I threw up my arm they swam off & jumped way high out of the water three times!

There was a long pause. Marina checked that she was still connected.

M: Da? You get bumped?

D: no

M: Are you mad at me?

D: no, i love it when my gf takes off for 2 mos

M: Well, I'm here now. Everyone else went to a party and I stayed here so we could have a chance to talk all night.

D: i don't really have that long to talk

M: What do you mean, you don't have long? I thought Saturday nights were going to be our guaranteed-no-matter-what-IM-night.

D: something came up

M: What do you mean something came up?

D: guys rented out this condo up at smugglers for night skiing. some people coming for a party after

Marina watched the lines pop up in the box. Her eyes stung as each line hit her in the gut.

M: But it's our first Saturday.

D: we can just hook up 2moro nite

M: So, you're already ditching me?

D: who ran off to play with dolphins?

M: Well, you're the one who decided not to go to U of H. We should be picking out Ala Moana dorms right now instead of IMing from a thousand miles away.

D: fine my fault

Marina took a deep breath to calm her frustration. She tried to pick the most diplomatic words to explain herself.

M: No, I'm not saying that. Just that giving that up will be hard. If I'm going to do it, I want to know what I'm missing. Vermont Community College isn't exactly known for its marine biology program.

Marina stared at the blank screen for a long time. Finally the blip at the bottom showed Damon typing.

D: guys honking. gotta go

M: No wait, don't do this. Let them go, stay with me and let's talk it out.

D: not up for all this drama right now

M: Damon, please don't leave it like this.

D: chill. we're fine. meet you tomorrow noon. laters

M: Wait. Da? But I can't meet tomorrow afternoon. I'll be working with the dolphins all day. I want to work this out with us. I swear I do.

Marina waited for Damon to come back on, but the screen stayed blank. Finally, she slammed her laptop shut.

She knew he didn't understand her fascination with marine biology. His eyes sort of glazed over when she'd talk about her afternoons at the hatchery. But how could he not *get* how cool it was to spend time with dolphins? And knowing that showing tourists how intelligent they were would make a positive impact on the way people treated the environment made it even more rewarding.

She knew Damon didn't care about ecology. When it came to attending the University of Hawaii, he had just been excited to try out surfing. He said it sounded like snowboarding. With sharks. But other than that, Hawaii was her dream, and Damon was just going along for the ride. But they'd been planning this together for three years. Why should she feel guilty for wanting to stick to the plan even when he had abandoned it?

Blowing her off on their first Saturday apart for some ski kegger was not cool. Marina stared hard at Dude. He might be a mammal, but she really felt like turning him into a flying fish. She stuffed him under her bunk instead.

She had given up a Welcome to the Bahamas party, and for what? To get blown off for a few turns down a ski hill and a boozer party afterward? Just great. Well, screw Damon. If he was going to party, so was she. She *was* in the islands.

Marina strode over to the mirror, unbraided her hair, and fluffed it out all wild. She rifled through Jeanette's makeup, found the gloss and mascara she had worn that first morning, and went to work. She stood back and then moved closer to the mirror to inspect the job.

"Well, it's not up to Jeanette's standards, but not half bad," she said aloud to the cabin.

As Marina opened her cabin door and stepped into the hallway, Bob Marley blasted from the party area. Jeanette's voice came through during a break between songs.

"Okay, Ryan. Have you ever taken your cousin to prom? Now remember, gotta tell the truth, rules of the game."

Marina giggled. Poor Ryan.

"No!"

Ryan sounded suitably tortured, and Jeanette sounded

suitably amused. Marina closed the cabin door behind her and headed toward the party. She took a deep breath of the fresh sea air when she reached the deck. She caught sight of Simon and Kristen entwined and leaning on the boat rail in the opposite direction from the group. She gave a little half wave, but they were too occupied with each other to notice. Not surprising, it was kind of romantic with the moon shimmering on the ocean. At least she could catch the last bit of the party to take her mind off Damon.

"Okay, I pick Link. Have you ever kissed a French girl?"

Marina stifled a gag. Didn't need to guess who that was. The music came back on, and she missed Link's answer. The others were catcalling and laughing. She hoped he was really letting Rhee have it. She grinned. At least Link was too smart to fall for such a blatant attempt to—

Marina stopped short as she rounded the corner. He was letting her have it all right.

Marina forced a smile back onto her shocked face as she tried to avoid the sight of Rhee sitting on Link's lap on one of the chaises with her tongue stuck down his throat. Link came up for air, and he broke back into his easy smile until he met Marina's eyes.

She wasn't sure what her expression must have been, but his eyes widened and he half stood, dumping Rhee unceremoniously on her perfect French butt.

"Oh God, sorry, Rhee," Link said, and offered her a hand back up, though his eyes were still on Marina.

Rhee looked up at him with a pout. Her eyes followed his until she saw Marina. Then her red lipsticked mouth turned into a smug smile.

"How nice of you to join us, Marina."

Link scooted to one end of the chaise and offered his crooked smile.

"Wanna seat, Barbie?"

Marina looked at the red smear across his mouth and tried not to let her own fake smile go crooked.

Everyone seemed to be pairing off on the boat. And Link with Rhee? Disgusting. She walked over to the cooler and pulled out an icy can of mango juice.

"No thanks, I'm just gonna grab a drink and head back."

She really wanted to put the can on her forehead to cool down, but she couldn't let Rhee see that she had gotten to her. So she cracked it open, took a big swig to stop the ache in the back of her throat, and headed back down to the cabin.

Seeing Rhee kissing Link also brought up unpleasant thoughts about Damon's after-ski party. She knew there'd be loads of girls there hanging on all the guys. She didn't think Damon would be the type to cheat, but the other guys would be trashing Marina for leaving, and they'd all be loaded. The thought of a predatory girl like Rhee zoning in on Damon made her shudder. She got into her bunk and squeezed her eyes tight to push away the image.

Chapter Nine

By the time Marina got back to the boat from the dolphin facility the next afternoon, Jeanette was already spread across the top bunk tapping away on Marina's laptop. Marina had given her free rein on the machine since Jeanette seemed to need to write home a lot, and Marina knew she'd be out most of the day.

"Sorry, just finishing up relaying a minute-by-minute account of my day to my jailor. I am thousands of miles away and still feel like he is standing over my shoulder. I hate it," Jeanette said.

"Is it really so bad?"

"Yes. Awful. He wants details of what I do all day long. I have to spend more time writing about my day than living it."

"So why don't you claim Internet problems and just leave it until tomorrow?" Marina asked.

"I can't. He'd be frantic. No, I'll just suck it up and relay a dad-approved day."

Marina flopped onto her bunk and kicked off her flip-flops.

"So you just lie?"

"Well, I would. But I got stuck with boring Ryan again, so it actually was a dad-approved day."

Jeanette handed down a bag of Skittles. Marina poked around and found a few red ones and chewed while thinking about that.

"I like Ryan."

"You would."

"Hey, what's that supposed to mean?"

"Nothing. He just is more your sort of people than mine," Jeanette said.

Marina stiffened. She wasn't exactly thrilled at the comment, considering Jeanette rarely said Ryan's name without some insult attached to it. She handed the bag up when Jeanette looked over and smiled.

"Just kidding, *Damarina.*" Jeanette raised one eyebrow as she handed the laptop down.

Marina took her laptop and then quickly retreated back

under the bunk to avoid Jeanette's questioning look.

"I wasn't snooping or anything. Your man IM'd. The window just popped up," Jeanette said.

"Oh?" Marina's face burned.

"When he came on looking for you, he signed off 'Still Damarina, right?' Awwwww." Jeanette dissolved into hysterics.

Marina was stuck between the embarrassment from the cheesiness of the nickname and relief that things really did sound okay again with Damon. He wouldn't be e-mailing trying to make up if he just hooked up with someone else at a party. "Can I ask a favor, Jeanette? I'm trying to figure out some stuff about me and Damon. Work things out in my head, you know? I just don't want to deal with people—"

"'Nuff said. Don't even sweat it, I won't say a word. It's your business, not anyone else's."

"Thanks."

Jeanette's legs appeared over the bunk, and she dropped down to the floor. "So anyway, *Damarina*, he came looking around lunchtime. Don't worry, I told him you were busy with José, the cabana boy."

Marina laughed. "Great, bet he loved that one."

Jeanette walked over to the wall mirror and put on some lipstick. "Just kidding. I told him you were doing school stuff and would be online tonight."

"Thanks."

"School stuff with a gorgeous half-naked white-water-raft guide from Australia, that is."

"Jeanette!" Marina launched Dude at her.

Jeanette giggled and dodged the stuffed dolphin on her way out the door.

On the morning of day eight, Marina's mind wandered during the lecture. She had been up late researching her essay topic and was tired. And they had covered most of this information the day before at the facility. Domenico was catching up those who weren't there. She couldn't believe they had already been in Nassau for a whole week. To earn TripTask points, some of the students had chipped in by reading the narration for the dolphin shows. Others had put on snorkel gear and pulled long thin weeds called turtle grass out of the net wall of the dolphin pens.

The focus research team had been tied up with accompanying the trainers on their rounds and learning how to take care of captive marine mammals. Marina was amazed when her trainer showed her the jagged white marks on the side of the small female dolphin he was feeding. The white skin was a different texture from the smooth rubbery gray skin because it was scar tissue. That dolphin had been attacked by a shark when it was a baby and had survived. The facility also helped rehabilitate injured dolphins.

Domenico was winding up the lecture, and she pulled

herself back into it as he spoke about the origins of dolphins and whales.

"While you might assume that dolphins and whales evolved from some sort of sea life, it may surprise you that they actually came from prehistoric wolves. The wolf-like creatures, in order to compete for dwindling food sources, had to go deeper and longer into the water on the coastline. Eventually, their capacity for swimming and holding their breath increased and their need for hind legs decreased. They evolved into modern-day dolphins," Domenico said.

There were skeptical and surprised murmurs among the sixteen students until Domenico pulled out an X-ray of one of the dolphins.

"See here? This little bone back by their hip never entirely disappeared when they stopped having functional legs."

"And that concludes today's session. Can my focus group meet me for a minute?"

Marina and Link slid out of the booth and joined Sam and Maaike.

"I know you guys have been at somewhat of a disadvantage for extra-credit work, with all the hours you have been putting in at the facility. So if you would like, you can join us this morning in preparing the dolphins' food in the fish house and earn some TripTask points. Go ahead and grab a set of old clothes if you are interested. See you at the facility at ten," Domenico said.

Marina headed to her cabin and went through her things while thinking about the first week at the facility. It had flown by.

After their first Saturday fight, she and Damon had both put in more effort at regular IM'ing. Marina tried a few times to tell Damon about some of the cooler things she was doing. He really was making an effort to be okay with her being away, but he still seemed bored with the conversation. So she just let it drop and listened to his stories about the mountain and the boys instead. It was her way of making an effort, too.

More and more, Marina caught herself surfing the Net in another window in the background as they chatted. She was finding it harder to have meaningful conversations with him, and she had trouble even remembering what they used to talk about all the time. She hoped that it was just the distance and that, once she got home, it would all be back to normal.

She didn't know what their chances would be if she did go on to the University of Hawaii without him. Secretly, she saw this as a test of how their long-distance relationship might be. And if it was a test, she felt like they were in serious danger of failing.

● ● ●

As she neared the dolphin facility, Marina could see Maaike, Sam, and Link waiting for her on the dock. She was cutting it close at three minutes to ten, but she loved that the facility was just a long walk down the beach. She preferred it to the short bus ride, which took almost as long with all the tourists zipping around on mopeds and clogging the roads. She hadn't had much of a chance to lounge in the Bahamas, so she hoped the next port would have these sugary white beaches, too. She had been to the coast of Maine every summer, but the sand there was golden brown and grainy, if not full of tiny pebbles and rocks. But this sand was soft, and the water was so clear she could watch the fish dart around from where she stood on the beach.

Link saw her coming and waved. Marina returned his smile and sat down next to Maaike. They had settled into a surprisingly comfortable team during the first week at the facility. She and Maaike compared their deepening tans while they waited for Domenico to call them over to the fish house.

After hosing off their legs to remove excess sand or dirt and handing around a bottle of antibacterial soap, which they used to wash up to their elbows, Domenico showed them into a large, well-constructed shed. Half a dozen trainers worked efficiently over stainless steel counters and huge sinks. The walls, floors, and ceiling were covered in shiny white linoleum. It all smelled faintly of bleach.

The sinks were full of water in which large rectangular blobs floated under the trainers' quick hands. A large ice machine sat at the back next to doors for two walk-in freezers. As she stared wide-eyed, a trainer loaded down with two huge plastic bags came out from one of the freezers. He walked over to a sink full of water and slit the plastic open, dumping in the contents.

"Bycatch," Domenico explained.

"Like from fishing boats?" Link asked.

"Shrimp boats, actually. From the Jamaican banks. They take what seafood they can sell and dump most of the rest in the sea. There are certain types of fish that we can use, so we buy the rest—whatever they can flash freeze before it goes bad—and we sort through it for dolphin food."

The trainers at the sinks were picking at the frozen fish, peeling them off the frozen block and placing them, one by one, on the silver counter. Another trainer picked it up, flipping it over to look for any scrapes or punctures. If it was whole and unblemished, he would peel open the blood-red gills on the side of the fish to smell the inside.

Domenico walked over and picked up a fish to show them how it was done.

"Can't have any marks; they would let in bacteria from the shrimp boats. It needs to smell fresh, or it's no good. We toss it."

He pointed to the huge trash bins rapidly filling with fish.

"Maybe three out of ten make the cut. Dolphins eat only live fish out in the sea, so they know they'll be good. Here, they eat what we give them. Their health depends on us. That is why you'll be pouring ice on top of the coolers and helping defrost the fish blocks. Leave the sorting to us."

Marina nodded. Sorting was a huge responsibility, and she was relieved to avoid it. She would feel horrible if a dolphin ate a bad fish and got sick because of her.

Domenico introduced them to the trainers at the sinks; they greeted the students with smiles and showed them how to pull out the fish and let the ice chunks melt off without sticking themselves with too many fins. It took practice, and Marina got painful little pricks now and again for the first hour. She and Link worked together at one double sink, and Maaike and Sam were across the shed at another. When the last bag was pulled from the freezer and sifted through hours later, she was exhausted.

"That was a lot of work. You do that every day?" Marina asked Domenico on her way out.

He and the others laughed. Marina colored and looked to Link to see what she had said.

"That was just for their lunch!" said Domenico.

Marina's mouth fell open.

"Life of a trainer—it's all part of it," he added.

Life of a dolphin trainer, indeed. They had been spoiled so far, doing only the fun stuff at the facility, petting the animals, playing with them, even getting in the water and swimming around watching them through snorkel masks. But seeing the work behind the scenes only made her more interested in marine biology. It felt even better to earn the fun stuff by doing hard work. It made it more meaningful. Her glamorous ideas of what it would be like to work at Sea World seemed sort of childish now.

They had the rest of the day free, so she said her good-byes to the others and headed into town to meet up with Jeanette and Ryan. She was surprised at the historic-looking government buildings she passed on the narrow streets on her way to Prince George Wharf. With their colonial style and black metal grid work, they looked more like what she'd expect in London than on an island in the Bahamas. Except these were washed with a light pink color like the inside of a shell.

Two massive cruise ships were docked at the wharf. Festival Place, the little village filled with shops and food kiosks, was congested with tourists. Marina was worried she might miss her roommate in the crowd, but then she heard the music coming from an indoor courtyard.

She made her way toward the sound and caught sight of Jeanette trying to pull Ryan out from the edge of the crowd to dance. Ryan was resisting, but from fifty yards away she could see the determination in her roommate's eyes.

The band played "goombay" music. Marina had read in a brochure how this African Bantu word for "rhythm" was used to describe the rake and scrape bands that dated

back to the days of slavery. Here, one man played maracas and had a pair of rhythm sticks tucked in the pocket of his baggy shorts. Another played on a goombay drum made from a barrel covered with goatskin. Marina had passed some stands selling them on her way into the Festival Place. An electric guitar looked odd played next to a man scraping a long carpenter's saw with a metal file. Some of the tourists were boogying freestyle, but the performers on the floor were doing an organized polkalike dance.

Marina stood on her toes and waved. A relieved Ryan saw her and pulled Jeanette out of the clearing and toward her side of the plaza. By the time they reached her, Jeanette and Ryan were arguing. What a surprise.

"I'm just saying—" Ryan said with his hands up in defense.

"I know what you're saying," Jeanette snapped before turning her back on him. "Hey, Marina."

"What's up?" Marina asked.

"Oh, we were watching this jewelry-making demonstration earlier. The artist forms the pieces right in front of you! They also have guys weaving straw bags and hats, and they'll put your name on them. There are about forty artisans, but this place is too crazy to hang around right now. It figures we pick cruise ship day to check it out. They said it is way more laid back when the boats aren't in port."

"Jeanette, you don't have to ignore me. I just don't get

why anyone would mark up a perfectly fine body is all," Ryan insisted.

Jeanette glared over her shoulder at him.

"What a charmer. I'm taking my *perfectly fine* body back to the boat. You coming, Marina?"

"Sure, I guess. Ryan?"

"No, you go ahead. Look Jeanette, I didn't mean anything by—"

"Later, Lensboy."

Jeanette stomped away, with Marina trailing behind her.

"What was all that about?"

"Oh nothing. Just Ryan being Ryan. They were making these awesome silver dolphin earrings that look like they're jumping through your ear, and I asked the artist if they made turtles. They did, so I asked if they would work as a belly ring."

"And you're mad . . . 'cause they wouldn't?"

"No. I'm mad 'cause . . . I don't know. I had to sit and listen to a whole mutilating-my-body speech. Most guys think navel rings are sexy. Ryan's a drag. You know, after being around him this last week or so, Link and his player ways aren't looking so bad. I mean, as long as you know what you're getting, it's not like you would get hurt. At least you know what to expect, or, more important, what not to."

Marina's stomach felt queasy, like something was burning in a not very good way.

"Right?" Jeanette asked.

Marina swallowed hard. Her mouth had gone dry. She had been all in favor of Jeanette and Link hooking up at the start of the trip. But after the past week of spending eight hours a day having fun with the guy, she wasn't as keen on the idea for some reason.

"Well—" Marina started and then stopped, unsure what she was going to say.

Jeanette stopped suddenly and turned to inspect Marina with narrowed eyes. "Wait a sec, you're still all about *Damarina*, right? I mean, you and Link don't... you're not..."

Marina flushed. "No, no. Nothing like that. We're just friends," she stammered.

Jeanette raised an eyebrow.

"Really!" Marina said, feigning interest in a stand of hats. She picked one up and traced the embroidered dolphin logo on the front to avoid Jeanette's eyes. When she noticed it was an Aussie-style outback hat, she dropped it like it was on fire. Jeanette didn't stop giggling until they were nearly at the boat.

Chapter Ten

Marina swayed back and forth in a loosely woven hammock hung from two palm trees on the beach near the facility. After her final shift at the dolphin facility, she just wanted to take a break and relax. She had been so busy with her work that she hadn't had a chance to enjoy the beautiful Bahamian beach.

Tomorrow afternoon they would head to the small island of Utila, off the coast of Honduras, to study whale sharks. And their last morning in the Bahamas would be busy. Her big essay was due in class, and then she'd promised Jeanette a shopping trip to the local craft market. But this

afternoon, she just wanted to be alone to relax and let the dolphin experience soak in.

She was slipping in and out of a doze when she saw Link running down the beach toward her.

"Baby!"

Link's voice echoed down the beach as he ran. She had to admit, the guy sure knew how to run. The sight was a nice addition to the already gorgeous scenery. She looked behind her to see who Link's "baby" was, but Rhee wasn't in sight. She turned around and sat up. She was the only one around at all.

"Baby! Baby, come quick!"

Marina blushed, was he calling her? Something in her stomach jumped, and her heart started racing. He was! Here was a gorgeous guy running down a white sand beach, grinning and calling her "baby." Sexist maybe, but it was totally Link-like. He meant no harm.

She slipped out of the hammock and stood. Maybe it was the emotional roller coaster of leaving the island, but she let real life drift away and ran to meet him. He was saying something else now. She couldn't make it out. They reached each other and Link swung her up and around in a hug laughing. It felt so right that she almost stumbled in shock when she recognized the feeling. She hadn't felt this way since the early days with Damon. Actually, she wasn't sure if there was ever this much thrill and warmth, even in the beginning of their relationship.

How could she have missed it? She liked Link! No wonder the thought of Link and Jeanette or Link and Rhee or Link and anybody felt so awful to think about. She liked Link, and he liked her. They were going to kiss. She wasn't sure how or why it was happening, but she could feel it. Link pulled her back down, put both hands on her shoulders, and looked straight into her eyes. She braced herself.

"Marina. She had the baby! Gracie had the baby!"

Marina's mouth dropped.

"I know, it's a shocker! Here we are waiting and waiting and then we are one day from leaving, and there it is. Don't know the sex yet, it happened about an hour ago. They separated the older males into the exit pens until the baby gets bigger. Guess they like to rough up the newcomers."

Marina's brain was trying to process what was happening. She was grateful Link mistook her shock for, well, shock. She was such an idiot. She could just die. Thank God she hadn't kissed him. That would have made this situation a lot more humiliating.

"Marina! Snap out of it. We gotta get back there. We can go right up to the enclosure and see the baby! Domenico talked to Marco. They need extra teams for something called BabyWatch. It will even count for TripTask points."

"Are you serious? The baby is really here?" she managed at last.

She laughed at his excited nod. Part of her was enjoying

the thrill of a lifetime. A real live, just-born baby dolphin! Her cheeks hurt from grinning. She was tearing up again, but in happiness this time.

A deeper part of her was still stunned. She really, really had wanted to kiss Link. There was no denying it now. She was a horrible person. A horrible girlfriend. And yet—Link was standing there holding her hand like it was the most natural thing in the world. Granted, Link was mostly holding her hand to pull her down the beach.

"Come on! No one else knows yet; we can sign up for at least two shifts of BabyWatch. We'll get one during the day and another tonight. There was still a two-to-four A.M. open when I left."

She took a deep breath and pushed away all thoughts of liking Link. The baby dolphin was the most exciting thing that had ever happened to her. Nothing was going to ruin it!

"Wait, what's a *BabyWatch*?" she asked as she struggled to keep up with his pace.

"They need to watch the baby twenty-four/seven for the first few weeks. Adult dolphins can stay underwater for fifteen minutes or whatever before they have to breathe, but the babies have to come up every thirty seconds. So if its tail fluke or fins get caught in a net, someone's got to help it back out. Wanna sign up?"

She needed to get her hand out of his before he noticed how sweaty it had gotten.

"Sounds good. Race ya," she said, and pulled away from Link.

Marina shivered. It was weird being in the dolphin facility at night. She was sitting up in the wooden watchtower on the key that overlooked the large enclosure. It was where they had been swimming around in snorkel gear that afternoon, but it seemed unfamiliar in the moonlight.

There was another team of trainers positioned at the other end of the football field–sized area. One of the trainers was following the mother and baby with a spotlight as they swam around. Marina was grateful for that. It was hard to make out any of the dozen or more dolphins in the slinky black water, much less pick out which one had a three-foot-long little one next to it. She heard the ladder creak as Link climbed up the tower and settled in next to her.

"Here's a coffee. Sweatshirt, too," he said.

Marina accepted them with a smile and put on the sweatshirt. Who would have guessed you'd need a sweatshirt in the Bahamas. But who would think you'd be sitting around at two in the morning watching dolphins swim, either.

"Can you tell what's going on?" she asked.

"Nope. I figure if there is anything wrong, the staff will tell us what to do," he said.

"Yeah, glad they didn't leave us by ourselves out here.

In the daytime it was way easier to see the baby. So tiny and perfect."

They sat and sipped their coffees.

"It's peaceful. Nice night," he said.

"Mmmm," Marina agreed, and took another swallow.

"So tell me about yourself, Marina. Who do you have missing you at home?"

She nearly sputtered the coffee. "Oh. No one," Marina lied instinctively.

She was glad for the dark to cover her guilty face. She had written an e-mail to Damon after dinner. They were best friends, and knowing the attraction she felt for Link, she couldn't sneak around behind Damon's back. But seeing in black and white that she wanted to break up made her queasy, so she saved it to her draft folder. It seemed horrible to break up in an e-mail. That there was already someone else made it even worse, so she decided to sleep on it. Or not, considering she was here and not actually sleeping. It was hard to deal with this stuff so far from home.

"No one? That's hard to believe," said Link.

Marina bit her lip. He knew about Damon. Maybe Jeanette had said something.

"Why? What do you mean?"

"Well, your parents must miss you," Link said.

"Oh! Well, yeah. Them. Or actually, I don't know, maybe

not. We all sort of do our own thing. I mean, they don't put much effort into being part of my life," she explained.

"Do you put any into being part of theirs?" Link asked.

Marina shot him an amused look. "No—I mean, it's not a problem for us. It's just the way our family works. I guess we just have different interests."

"Sorry. I didn't mean that in a bad way. I was just thinking about my situation," Link said.

"What's your family situation like?" asked Marina.

"Well, about a year ago, I got really involved with rafting, at the expense of other things in my life. It's so hard when you have a real passion for something not to blow off everything else. You know?"

Marina couldn't help but think of Damon and the ski team. She'd never thought that skiing might be for him what marine biology was for her.

"Anyway, I had a lot of knock-down-drag-outs with my mom about it. She wanted me to quit rafting until I graduated. It got so bad, I moved out and in with some guides. For a while, I never went home. But eventually we set up dinners, and I'd go hang with my little sister—she's nine— warn her about boys, help braid her hair," he laughed and flipped up Marina's braid.

"I came around and cut back my river days. Moved back in a few months ago, and decided to go on this trip to show my intention to be a serious student. Or at least

to be a student. The university saw it my way, and they are overlooking my poor performance this past fall and letting me in next year."

"Sounds like you really sorted everything out," she said, impressed.

They shared the companionable silence for several moments. Link sat back. Their shoulders touched, and they sort of leaned into each other. It felt comfortable, easy. With Link being such a natural flirt, it was hard to tell what he was feeling. Occasionally a dolphin would come to the surface and spout with a faint whoosh sound.

"It's crazy about dolphins, huh?" Marina said at last.

"What about them?"

"That whole sleeping thing. They are swimming around down there in the middle of the night on autopilot, one brain hemisphere totally knocked out, the other zooming around awake. Can you imagine sleeping with half a brain at a time?" she marveled.

Link thought for a moment.

"Dunno. Maybe ask Tali how it feels?"

Marina cracked up and swatted him.

"You are so bad!"

"I know," he said with a laugh. "Be right back."

Link handed her their waterproof flashlight and climbed down.

Marina sat in the dark and listened to the rhythmic whooshing of the dolphins spouting below her as they came up for air. The wooden boards of the tower weren't comfortable, and her leg was going to sleep. She changed positions and thought about her talk with Link.

Link had straightened himself out. He'd made family a priority even while keeping focused on his passion. Maybe Damon was trying to do the same thing. He wanted to stay close to his mom, and he didn't want to let go of his passion for skiing. And he shouldn't either. He'd been skiing since he was four in Colorado, and he went every chance he could after moving to Stowe. She had never taken it seriously, because to her it was just skiing. Her asking him to move to Hawaii suddenly felt as selfish as his asking her to stay in Vermont. How had she never seen that before?

She suddenly heard splashing to her left. She first thought it was Link playing around, until she saw the spotlight swing over to the right below her tower. It shone through the water and flashed on a small wiggling object a few feet below. It was the baby!

"Get her out, she's in the net!" One of the trainers yelled.

Marina jumped up and flew down the ladder, skinning her shin as she went. She felt the spotlight on her as she tripped along the boardwalk, half crawling to where the splashing was coming from. Oh God, oh God, oh *God*! What was she supposed to do?

Link was nowhere. The other trainers were yelling and running for her, but they were at the opposite end of the

enclosure. They'd never get there in time. How much of the thirty seconds had already passed? The baby couldn't hold its breath much longer. She took a last frantic look around, then realized it was up to her. Holding her breath, she looked down into the inky water and jumped.

Chapter Eleven

Marina was lucky they were on the section closest to the island and the water was only chest high. Even so, with the heavy soaked sweatshirt and tennis shoes on, she felt like she was pushing toward the baby in slow motion. The other trainers' yells were drowned out by the fierce splashing a few feet from Marina's outstretched hands. She felt a chill colder than the night sea slide through her as she realized the baby was fighting for its life. She closed her eyes from the burning saltiness and reached down, groping blindly.

The wet rubbery dolphin slipped through her hands.

She took a deep breath and went under to get a better grip. Marina managed to slide an arm around the struggling creature, and she felt down its back to the tiny fluke. Its triangular tail had somehow poked through a square of netting, and it was pulling with the two pointy ends on the outside of the enclosure. She came up and gasped. If she could only pull the baby back a bit and then to the side to free one of the fluke tips, but the baby was following its instinct to flee.

As she headed back under to try again, a hulk of animal body shoved her back and knocked her over. It was the mother. It probably thought Marina was going to hurt the baby! Another splash startled her, and she felt someone push between her and the mother. She groped and found the baby's tail fluke. She used every bit of her strength to move the baby backward and tug it to the side until the net released it. With one strong push, the baby was off and free, heading up to breathe. Someone was struggling with the mother, though, and the protective animal body-checked Marina's savior before taking off after her calf.

Marina looked up through blurred, salty eyes and saw the two trainers. One was radioing for help. The other dropped to his stomach on the boardwalk and offered her an arm. As she was scraped over the side to safety, she realized that both trainers were in front of her and not in the water. She looked back at the enclosure. Link was moaning and floating with one arm held tight against his side. The trainer gasped and hopped into the sea. He lifted Link, and, with the other trainer's help, they got him up onto the boardwalk. Link groaned and rolled to one side.

"Oh my gosh, are you okay?" Marina crawled over to him.

Her teeth were chattering, and she barely noticed when the other trainer pulled off her sopping sweatshirt and replaced it with a dry towel. The whine of a boat motor from the facility started. The trainer pushed her back, and they inspected Link with the flashlight. A grimace replaced his normal crooked smile, and Marina felt her eyes burn with more than salt water.

"Broken ribs?" one trainer asked the other.

"Could be, maybe collarbone, too," the other said.

"Broken, something's broken?" Marina heard the panic in her voice.

"Are you okay, Marina?" Link rasped out.

"Me? I'm fine. Oh my God, you're asking about me? Are *you* okay?"

"Good. Fine," he gasped.

The boat slid up to the dock, and Domenico hopped up, giving a hand to a man carrying a small bag. The man—a medic—knelt, rummaged in his bag for a pair of scissors, and cut off Link's sweatshirt. His hands prodded around Link's side and back, causing Link to groan louder. The man nodded and rattled something in a low voice. Together Domenico and the medic lowered Link into the

boat, then it sped off within seconds. Marina sat on the dock in a daze. Domenico stayed back with her and put his arm around her in a clumsy hug.

"Your man'll be fine," he reassured her.

Marina let the "your man" pass. No, this wasn't her boyfriend. This was just a guy who risked his health to save her.

"But where are they taking him?" she managed.

"They'll take him to the hospital to do X-rays and check for internal injuries."

"Internal injuries," Marina whispered.

Domenico patted her back as they heard the approach of another boat. "These dolphins are beautiful, but they are wild animals. The mother didn't mean to hurt him. She was protecting her young. Thank you for saving the baby."

Marina couldn't speak. The idea of "internal injuries" was floating around in her head. She looked up as the boat approached. Marco was on board, summoned by radio, no doubt. They took her straight back to the dive boat in the small skiff. She was silent during the trip along the shore, and she gripped Link's cut-apart sweatshirt in her hands. Marco helped her onto the back deck.

"You'll be okay? I need to go to the hospital. They are just checking him out as a precaution. I talked to the doctor. I'm sure he's just fine."

Marina nodded. She watched the dinghy speed away and sat on one of the back benches on the deck. She stared at the sea and the dark shoreline. She tried to make her mind focus on her dolphin essay—whether to write about the subtle difference between spinner and spotted dolphins or on the sleeping habits of dolphins—just to keep it off worrying about Link. But the sound of the splash when Link jumped in to save her echoed in her head. She waited there until the sky began to glow pink, but they still hadn't returned. Finally, Marina slowly climbed the steps to her cabin. She fell into her bunk and quickly sank into an exhausted sleep.

When Marina woke she was totally out of it. And sore. Her muscles ached.

Jeanette sat on the floor of the cabin reading a magazine. She jumped up when she noticed Marina looking at her. "Are you okay?" Jeanette asked.

Marina sat up and pushed her legs over the edge of the bunk with a groan. "Yeah, I guess so. How's—"

"He's fine. Nothing broken, just a bad bruise. But they gave him some pain stuff, and Ryan said he already crashed for the night."

"For the *night*? How long did I sleep?" Marina looked out the porthole. The sky was turning orange.

"Well, I thought I heard you come in around daybreak. So all day, I guess. Bet you're hungry. Marco said not to wake you at lunch."

"I missed the whole last day here!"

"I know, I'm sorry. But that was an amazing thing you did."

Marina's cheeks reddened. "I didn't really think about it. I just jumped in. It's not that big of a deal."

"I'd have been too scared. You're braver than me."

Marina laughed at the thought of being braver than her wild-child roommate.

"I got you a souvenir since you couldn't go shopping with me like we had planned," said Jeanette. She pulled out a bag and handed it to Marina.

Marina shuffled through the Bahamian newspaper filler and pulled out an olive-colored Outback-style sunhat. It had snaps on both sides to fasten up the brim. The front was embroidered with a familiar little dolphin jumping from the sea. It was the one she had been holding while talking about Link at the market. Jeanette was giving her a mischievous grin. Marina put it on and looked in the mirror.

"I love it!"

"It's perfect, isn't it! See, you couldn't have passed it up, could you?"

Marina grinned back at her. "Nope."

"Um, good. Because—" Jeanette sheepishly pulled out another bag and lifted a khaki one embroidered with a turtle. Marina laughed.

"'Cause I really wanted one, too, after I got yours. I'm not trying to pull a Rhee/Tali matching thing, though. I can just save it for at home if you'd rather I not wear it here."

Jeanette pushed hers down, and they checked out each other's reflection.

"No way. It's perfect on you," Marina assured her.

"Speaking of, you should have seen Rhee fawning all over Link when he and Marco got back. Like she was playing little wifey or something."

"Oh?"

"Yes. And then Ryan..."

Marina let Jeanette's chatter about Ryan's latest faux pas wash over her as she thought about the "little wifey" comment. So maybe that was the deal. Maybe Rhee and Link did have something going. How could anyone as great as Link see anything in Rhee? Well, other than the obvious. But he was better than that, wasn't he?

"So, are you coming?" Jeanette asked.

"Sorry, coming where?"

"It's time for dinner. We've already cleared Customs and Immigration, and we'll be leaving anytime. Come on down, you're a celebrity. Everyone is dying to hear about you saving the baby."

That sounded like the last thing in the world Marina wanted to deal with. She was confused about her feelings for Link and felt guilty about his getting hurt protecting her. Retelling the story of what happened wasn't too appealing.

"Um, I don't know if I'm really up for that."

Jeanette gave her a sympathetic smile. "If you want, I could just make you a plate? You could go on up to the chaise lounge area if you want some downtime."

"Thanks. That would be great."

Marina's arms and legs felt like lead as she slowly climbed the steps to the deck. She sat down in a chaise lounge and watched the last wisps of the sunset. The day before she felt like she'd learned so much during her stay. And she *had* learned a lot—about the dolphins. It was just herself she wasn't clear on yet. She listened to the chains and ropes being loosened as the engines rumbled to life and seemed to say good-bye to the silhouetted coast of the Bahamas.

Chapter Twelve

Utila, one of the Bay Islands off the coast of Honduras, was only a day's journey south from the Bahamas, but what a difference. The boat arrived at night, and when Marina woke up and went outside to the railing, she was surprised to find that the island was tiny, and flat, and hot. This area was better known for what was under the sea than above it, Marina had been told. She could see several pastel painted concrete hotel structures in the distance. Their boat was already tied to a small wooden dock. A matching wooden dive shop and restaurant with huge glass picture windows looked out onto the dock. The place was bustling

with early-morning divers preparing their gear. The dive shop acted as the sponsoring facility for the whale shark tagging project that Simon and Kristen were doing.

Marina's muscles were still stiff as she gingerly walked into the dining room for some breakfast. Jeanette, Ryan, Si, and Kris were already in the booth.

"They look like whales, but they're really sharks?" Jeanette was asking.

"Yep. Sharks. But they have that baleen thing so they eat mostly plankton or the tiniest of fish," Si began "so they are no danger to be around. Except—"

"Except they range from thirty-five to fifty feet long. And you gotta respect anything that's bigger than the dive boats we're on," Kris finished.

Marina shivered and took a long sip of coffee. She was trying to keep an open mind, but swimming with sharks the size of three cars put together was freaking her out a bit. Especially after seeing what only a seven-foot dolphin could do to you. Maybe she could work her way up by diving with a nice little three-foot-long shark or something.

Marco walked in and looked over his clipboard. Everyone was there except for Link, who was still recovering, and, once again, Tali.

"Rhee? Your roommate?" Marco asked.

"Vomiting again. It happens every time we go on a long trip," Rhee said, while sucking on a lollipop.

Marco looked concerned.

"I'll give her some extra hints. I didn't know she was having such a hard time."

"I have some candied ginger she could try. My friends back home are all yachters. They say it does wonders for rough seas," Simon offered.

Rhee held up her sucker with a smile. "Pregnancy sweets. You know, the ones women use to get rid of the sickness of the morning? They work just as well and don't taste horrible like the ginger."

"And that's not working for her either?" Marco asked.

Rhee looked at him blankly. "Oh. Well, I do not know. I only brought enough for me."

Marco looked down at his clipboard with raised eyebrows. "Send her to me, I'll see what I can do. And thank you, Simon, for the generous offer. It's nice that Tali has a friend on board."

Rhee didn't even blush at the comment.

Marco cleared his throat and began the orientation.

"Welcome to Utila. The island is small, only twelve miles long, so you really ought to get a feel for it during our two weeks here."

"Point me to the beach," Rhee said with a smile.

"No beaches," Marco said.

Marina noted his satisfaction with Rhee's dismayed look.

"Well, what sort of Caribbean island is this with no beach?" she protested.

"An island rich with history and abundant unspoiled reef to explore."

Ryan raised his hand. "Are we all going to have access to some diving here, or just those on this focus project?"

"We have an agreement with the lodge. You may go, space available, on as many dives as you like while we are here. Let me get the director so he can tell you about what the island has to offer. He's the expert."

Everyone was whispering and chatting while Marco was gone. Ryan flipped through a fish-identification book, pointing out local species to Jeanette. Simon and Kris were laughing as they argued over which of them remembered a Swahili phrase correctly. Marina picked at her notebook. She felt Link's absence from the table.

Seeing the other couples reminded her of some unfinished business she needed to take care of. When she could get Marco alone, she was going to ask about where to find a phone. She couldn't e-mail Damon, so it was time to call him. Maybe if she could get up the nerve to do that, swimming with a forty-foot shark would be easy.

Marco came back with a short, shaggy-haired local. His age was impossible to guess. His skin was dark, his hair a sun-bleached orangish red, and his eyes were light aqua. He smiled at everyone—particularly the girls—Marina noticed. He started with an animated speech about whale sharks. At least she thought it was about whale sharks. She couldn't understand a word he was saying.

"Is he speaking Spanish?" Jeanette whispered.

"I don't think so," Marina whispered back.

The students were all giving one another looks, but the director seemed oblivious to their confusion. Marina was really embarrassed for them all, until she saw Marco trying to cover a smile. The director seemed to be winding up.

"Okay?"

He looked around at the students, who mumbled "okay" but didn't meet his eyes.

"Captain Ron, here. And can anyone tell me the language I was just speaking?" the director asked.

There was a collective sigh of relief. And they all laughed and admitted being clueless.

"No? No one? It is what we folk around here call... English," he finished after a pause. He burst out with a booming laugh. "Island English is a mixture of all the different languages and accents that have passed through our island. We had the Garifunas, the West Indians, the Carib Indians, every European pirate and explorer you could imagine along with his crew. Some stay, some go, but they all leave a bit of their speech behind, yah? But don't worry, we usually speak that way just to each other. For you, we have gringo English. Take no offense by 'gringo,' none is meant. And you'll be hearing the term everywhere."

"So let's talk about the whale sharks. Biggest fish in the world. And Utila has the most of anywhere in the world, year-round. Some place in Australia has them, but only

three months a year. Utila's so nice they stay and stay and stay. People from everywhere want to come see a whale shark. So we tag them so we can make the big tips."

Marina was shocked until she caught the twinkle in his aqua eyes.

"No, no, no. Don't write that down in your little notebooks. Joking, joking. We care. These are amazing animals. No one ever knew they existed until some fifty years ago. The sharks dive down a thousand feet or so. Guess how we know? We tag 'em. Some of you might tag one if we get lucky. We learn about them to protect them."

Captain Ron gave them another big smile. Marina felt a pang of envy that Simon and Kristen would be hanging out with such a character for their project.

"Anyone here like diving? We have some excellent sea walls to dive alongside, with chances to see some big sea life. Write this down, 'pelagic.' That means the critter travels the open ocean rather than living in one spot, lounging lazylike on the beach. Big things: manta rays, blacktip sharks, and, of course, Utila's claim to fame, the whale shark."

Marina grinned at Jeanette. Even if the whale shark was a bit intimidating, she couldn't wait to go under and see more than the elusive Oldsmobile fish of Lake Champlain.

"Let me get my two focus groups going. You run and get your bags. That boat with yours truly, Captain Ron, behind the wheel leaves in, say, fifteen minutes. We're gonna go look us some whale sharks, people! So let's go, go, go!"

Captain Ron clapped his hands military style. Si and Kris slid out with a chuckle and ran for the exit behind six other students. Someone started clapping, and they all joined in to applaud his speech.

He beamed at them. Captain Ron spun and gave a deep bow before jaunting up the steps and off the boat. He did have the air of a pirate about him. He could have had a hook on one hand, and it would have seemed entirely natural.

Tali passed him on her way into the dining area. She stumbled to her table, and shuddered at the sight of all the leftover food. Marina felt sorry for the girl. She'd heard that when you were seasick you felt like you could die. Or maybe just like you *wanted* to die, from the looks of Tali.

"Okay, people," Marco began, "I'll ask Captain Ron about TripTasks for this port—"

"Who has the most points?" Rhee interrupted.

"Well, while there is a possible incentive for the top students, your focus should be on your research papers, and on learning and getting the most out of this trip. Not trying to outdo each other for points. So I've decided to keep your point totals private. Whether or not you take on a task should be because you want to enrich your travels."

Everyone groaned. That was all fine and good, but it would be torture not to know how close or far you were from everyone else.

"I will say, for those of you who haven't already heard, Marina and Link did an amazing thing the other night at the dolphin facility by saving the baby dolphin. Things of that nature deserve to be rewarded. So it should be no big mystery who is at the top of the list at the moment."

Marina couldn't contain her grin. Rhee's glare made his comment even sweeter.

"Doing things above and beyond, as Marina and Link did, making a serious contribution to the boat or the culture of the location we are visiting, will result in bonus points. And again, if you are creative and see an opportunity for a task that I have not, come to me, we can work something out. We are here to learn. And remember, those Trip Tasks are secondary, behind your essay and participation grades."

Marina caught Marco as everyone was leaving the orientation.

"Um, Marco? How is Link doing?"

"He's gonna be fine. Just bruised his ribs. All they could do was wind an Ace bandage around it, so he needs to take it easy for a while."

"Good." She breathed a sigh of relief. "Also, I need to call the States. Do you know where I'd go to do that?"

"You need to call home? 'Cause if it is an emergency, I can check to see if we can use Captain Ron's office phone. Is something wrong?"

"Oh, no, nothing like that. I just wanted to touch base

with a friend. Do their pay phones take local coins only?"

Marco laughed.

"Sorry, no pay phones. In fact, there are only phones in about one out of every thirty houses. Everyone just goes to those local houses and then they contact an operator to find out how much the call costs."

"You're kidding!"

"That's just how it is. They didn't even have electricity here until 1985 or so. Everyone had gasoline-powered generators before then."

"Oh, all right. I can just e-mail," Marina said.

She went back to her cabin and, stepping around Jeanette, who was sitting on the floor painting her toenails, Marina threw herself on her bunk. She sat holding Dude and tried to decide what to do. It was so frustrating. She'd made her decision to break up with Damon, but now she felt like she couldn't. She sighed heavily.

Jeanette looked up. "So, I hear everything on the island is closed today 'cause it's Sunday. But they have a band dance going on tonight."

"Sunday! It's Sunday? Oh crap, oh crap, oh crap—"

Marina jumped up and threw aside a pile of her things, looking for her computer under her bunk.

"What, what, what?"

"Nooooo," Marina groaned.

She couldn't believe she'd forgotten her Saturday-night IM session with Damon last night! It was understandable,

considering everything going on, but still. This was going to make the hurt of breaking up ten times worse. She was hoping they could talk reasonably and it might be a mutual thing. But not now. He was gonna be pissed. Way pissed. She powered up the laptop, hoping he might be online. The smiley next to his name was sleeping. She wanted to tell him what she was thinking, but to leave a message would be harsh. She typed out a quick e-mail.

From: Marinabiology@email.com
To: SkierBoi@email.com
Subject: Oops!

Damon,

I am sooooo sorry. The last couple days were wild. I saved a baby dolphin's life! Now that really sounds crazy, doesn't it? But it's true. I feel really bad that I missed our Saturday date. When can we meet on IM? Anytime, you name it. I'll be here. Okay? I really am sorry!

Marina

She had waffled about whether to sign it "Love, Marina" or just "Marina." She *did* love Damon. After everything they'd been through, she would always love him as a friend. But somewhere between going through his mom's illness and spending more time on their separate interests, things had changed between them. Senior year was coming, and decisions had to be made about the future. Really hard decisions.

After she'd settled on "Marina," she carefully closed the laptop lid with a click.

Jeanette looked up from painting her toes at the click. Their eyes met.

"Everything okay?"

"I like Link," Marina blurted.

Jeanette smiled and closed the bottle of nail polish. She moved in a clumsy wet toenail crawl over to Marina and hugged her. "I'm so glad you realized it before I had to point it out myself!"

"Really? Was I that obvious?"

"Well—yes. But only to me."

"I wrote Damon to meet on IM. I want to break up. Not for Link, exactly. I just see now that we are heading in different directions. Literally," Marina said.

"Are you happy?"

"Well, I mean…it's sad. He's been everything in my life for three years. But we are starting to hurt each other now. And that's even worse than breaking up."

Jeanette nodded.

"I'm going to do it on IM. E-mailing him without any warning is too mean," Marina said.

"I guess. But then again, I'd rather not have to get

dumped with the person watching me. I'd much rather get the e-mail. It's gonna hurt either way," Jeanette said.

"Maybe. I'll think about it. There wasn't even a message from him about my missing our date last night. Maybe he already suspects something," Marina said.

"You're coming tonight, though, right? Everyone is," Jeanette said.

"I guess. What's a band dance, anyway?"

Jeanette brought one foot up and blew on her toes to dry the polish.

"Dunno. Supposed to be some local band at a little bar. Everyone dances and has a party. They even fry a hog. Like, the whole thing. Crazy."

"Yeah, but a bar? Marco would never go for that."

"No, he's the one who suggested it."

"Would it be terrible for me to see if Link's coming?"

"Um, seeing as how the guy saved your life, I think that would be entirely appropriate."

Marina laughed as she left the cabin. "Oh, yeah. I should probably thank him for that!"

Chapter Thirteen

The band dance was held on a little plot of land by the sea. There was a teakwood bar under a thatched-roof overhang with a giant freezer behind it, running on a noisy generator. Other than that, the only structure was a low fence made of bound branches that surrounded a large patch of sand. It was already half filled with dancers of all ages when they arrived.

The music was great. It wasn't what she expected, no steel drums or anything, just three guys—one with a keyboard, another with an electric guitar, and a third on the microphone. The singer's voice was amazing, low and raspy but perfectly in tune. The music of choice consisted of some dance-hall tunes with double meanings that made Marina crack up at how outrageous the words were, some "companero," which Marco said was cowboy music from the Honduran mainland, and some old Johnny Cash country ballads.

Marina sat with Ryan and a very mellow Link near a domino table on one side of the bar. They watched Jeanette on the dance floor with her short curls flying as she was spun around and pulled back into the arms of her partner. Jeanette was laughing her head off, and Marina wondered where she got her confidence. Probably didn't hurt that once she'd accepted the first local guy's invitation to dance, she hadn't sat down since, trading partners each time the band played a different tune.

Rhee stood off to the side and looked bored. She looked bor*ing*, too. What a waste of an experience. Marina was glad to see that Tali had left her little leader and joined Teresa on the dance floor. Some of the other students were dancing, too, mostly with each other.

Link went and brought them back sodas.

"Marina? Can I tell you something?" Ryan asked.

"Sure," she said.

"I think your cabinmate is pretty cool."

If Link hadn't been sitting there, Marina might have answered, "I think yours is, too."

She smiled at Ryan in sympathy. She wasn't surprised,

since he always seemed to be hanging out with Jeanette despite her constant teasing. But for a guy like Ryan, it was a major confession. She held back her laugh. They were on the same boat and in the same boat. There was a salty spray in the air, and the suggestive music made her feel a little reckless. And a little Jeanette-like and confident, she hoped.

"You know what? Liking somebody is a good thing. It shouldn't be something to hide and pretend about."

She had to yell over the music that had started again. Ryan didn't look convinced. But she was. She was going to tell Link how she felt. She just had to find the right moment. They turned back to watch the domino game.

A pair of young locals were playing some middle-aged men at the domino table. The men laughed at each domino smacked on the table by the kids, and one of them kept leaning back to Marina and explaining the game. It was all about math, but these guys were like mind readers.

They watched as the game played out. The man's voice got louder as the turns came around again. He finished by slamming down his final domino so hard all the other dominoes jumped on the table.

"Key card!" he yelled in triumph, and both men hauled themselves up from their white plastic lawn chairs to give each other a double high five. The kids pushed back their chairs in disgust.

"Yeah, you go on, you go on, boy. I'll be an Old Head

before you'll ever be able to beat me! You hear?"

The men laughed and sat back, sipping their rum in victory while one of the new players swirled the ivory rectangles around with his hands in a shuffling motion.

"What's an Old Head?" Marina asked him.

"See there?" He pointed to a wizened old man sitting with some primly dressed middle-aged women. "He's an Old Head. Got the whole history of the place hidden up there behind all those wrinkles. Never did much for writin' it down back in the day, but he tell you all the stories of how things was and who came from where and what."

The old man looked to be about a hundred, but Marina could see the deference shown him by everyone there. He was surrounded by a crowd of kids darting around playing tag and wandering out on the dance floor.

"Darlin', you do me a favor? Go on over to that fire there and bring us some chicharon?"

"Um, sure," Marina said. She stood and left Ryan to his misery.

She found Marco chatting with Simon and Kristen about their day. Apparently it was a bust on the whale sharks, but they had seen some schools of tuna and sea birds, which was a good sign for tomorrow, since all three groups ate the same food. Kristen had danced a time or two with the boat driver and once with Captain Ron, but she stuck closer to Simon when she noticed it bothered him. Marina thought they were so cool together.

"Hey, Marco? The man over there asked me to get him a plate of chicharon?"

Marco hopped up with a smile and rubbed his hands together.

"Let's go for it. I haven't had chicharon in ages!"

Marco led Marina over to a group of men who were stoking an open wood fire. A huge kettle was propped up over it on some boulders, and it bubbled and spit with boiling grease. Two guys about Marco's age were taking turns stirring the contents with a long wooden paddle. Marina looked away from the sight of the giant hog carcass hanging from a mango tree. Two guys hacked away chunks of meat with a machete and put them on a tray to add to the pot before covering the carcass back up with a wet sheet to keep off the bugs and dirt.

"Hey, guys, got some chicharon ready yet?" Marco asked.

One of the boys went for a couple of plates and lifted the lid from a big pot on a makeshift table. The boy placed six or seven golden brown squares and triangles an inch or so thick on each plate. He hacked a few limes in half with a machete while Marina held her breath. He looked to be only nine or ten years old, but no one else seemed to think the massive knife was too dangerous for him. He handed the plates over with a smile.

Marina looked down, trying to figure out what chicharon was exactly. It didn't look like pork.

"Try it," Marco said.

Marina lifted a golden square and inspected it. It looked like some sort of toasted, fried something, with scores crisscrossed in a diamond pattern. Marco smiled and squeezed some fresh lime juice onto it. She lifted it to her mouth and bit into it.

It was hard. Very hard, very crunchy. And amazing. Sort of salty and with a tang from the lime. It tasted like the best chip she had ever had.

"Oh my *God*, what is this?" she moaned.

"Since you like it so much, I'll tell you. Fried pig skin," Marco said with a laugh.

If she didn't still have the incredible taste in her mouth, she might have been grossed out. Instead, she laughed and took another bite. Marco headed toward the domino table with a plate piled high and sent Marina back to Simon and Kristen with the other.

Kristen was just giggling and saying no to yet another local who wheedled her for a dance, pulling on her hand. He seemed to disregard the fact that an unhappy-looking Simon was standing with his arm around her. He finally gave up and went to dance with an island girl.

"You could have gone, you know. Just 'cause I don't dance—" Simon was saying.

"I'm fine, I'd rather hang with you," Kristen assured him.

Marina munched on a piece of chicharon and offered

the plate to Simon. Kristen picked it up and sniffed it.

"*Kitunguu*, Simon. Yep, this is meat," she said to Marina. "I've been a vegetarian for a few years now, and Si's trying it out so it will be easier for us when we are at school together."

"You guys are going to the same college?" Marina asked.

"One way or the other. We are applying in NYC and Auckland, so it'll be close to home for at least one of us. It just won't be the marine biology program we wanted if we go to a New York school."

"I'm applying to the marine bio program at the University of Hawaii," Marina said.

"I've heard that's a great program!" Kris said.

"Babe, I'm gonna go search down some food for you. I know I saw cabbage salad over there. Maybe they have something else, too," Si told her.

Kris watched him leave and then turned back to the dance floor. "God, Jeanette's having sooooo much fun!"

Marina watched a sweaty, smiling Jeanette accept a filled coconut with a long straw from the five-year-old with whom she had been dancing the last song. It was so cool how the parents brought their kids to the dance with them. Even the toddlers were shaking it on the sidelines.

"Simon said you could dance," Marina said.

"Well, yeah, but he'd feel lousy. Sometimes you just have to give up things to make the relationship work well.

What's a few dances when it comes to something that could be great forever? Everything takes work," Kristen said.

"But you make it look so easy!" Marina said.

"That's because it feels easy," Kristen replied.

Marina suddenly felt very lonely.

She noticed that Link and Ryan had moved over by the bar. She headed their way with the chicharon. The guys were pointing over at her roommate, looking concerned.

"Hey, Marina? Does Jeanette look kind of, um, wobbly, to you?" Ryan asked.

"Wow. Has she been drinking? She looks loaded," Link said.

"She wouldn't do that. Marco's right here. She's not stupid," Marina said.

Jeanette looked up at that moment and gave them a big wave. Too big. At some point she had kicked off her shoes. She left her partner mid-dance and weaved toward them barefooted. The bartender leaned forward.

"You talking about the gringa? Oh yeah, she's feeling happy. Been having my special Island Juice in the Coco all night," he said.

Jeanette's cheeks were bright pink, and her eyes were one step past sparkly to glassy. She was tanked, and she didn't even know it.

"I'll go get Marco and find her shoes," Ryan said.

Jeanette reached over and fell into Link's arms. Great. First Rhee, now Jeanette. Marina had to tell Link she liked him before every girl but her ended up in his arms.

"Link. I am so, so, so, so, so happy that Marina is gonna dump her boyfriend for you! You guys are great. Just great!" Jeanette singsonged.

Marina caught the initial look of shock before Link's eyes went cold. She turned to Link to explain, but he was already walking away. Fast. Marina closed her eyes and wished she could crumble into a pile of sand. She thought about running after him, but her feet were glued to the ground. She didn't know what she'd say if she caught him anyway. "Um, sorry I lied about being single." Or "You know when I said I just wanted to be friends? Good news! I changed my mind." She stood and watched Link stomp off in the direction of the boat.

After putting Jeanette to bed, Marina reluctantly opened her laptop. Now that Link hated her for hiding a boyfriend, there was no immediate need to break up with Damon long distance. She could wait until she got home if she wanted. But since she had made the decision to call things off, she found she didn't want to wait anymore—even if Link was upset with her.

She signed on and found that Damon had finally responded to her e-mail asking for an IM meeting.

From: SkierBoi@email.com
To: Marinabiology@email.com
Subject: (no subject)

Marina,

Hey. I don't think the IM thing is working out. The guys gave me hell when they found out you blew me off. And you barely write or ask about stuff here at home. Did you know that my mom had her one-year remission anniversary? So how come it's wrong that I don't get all hyped up about your marine biology stuff, but not wrong that you're not into what's going on with me? I think I need to spend a few days on the slopes alone to sort things through. Maybe doing our own thing the rest of the school year is a good thing. We can just pick back up this summer when we can be together again, right?

Da

Marina read the words with a sinking feeling. No. Not right. She had secretly hoped he might be feeling like she was. She hoped maybe he would even be the one to start the talk to end things. But now she couldn't even IM him to explain how she felt, especially not after she'd forgotten about his mom's milestone anniversary.

Marina drafted three e-mails but deleted them all. After everything they'd been through together, it seemed so cold to break things off with an e-mail. He was her best friend.

But it felt even worse letting her best friend sit and wait on something that was already over and that she knew in her heart wasn't coming back.

Marina hardly slept that night, with thoughts of Damon and Link running through her mind. She mentally rehearsed what she would say to Link the next morning at breakfast. She was in the dining room getting a pre-breakfast coffee to try to wake up when she saw someone coming down the kitchen ladder. From the muscled calves and oh-so-nicely fitting khaki shorts she could tell it was Link. She froze trying to figure out what to say to make the situation less awkward.

Link turned as his feet hit the last rung and almost fell on his face when he saw Marina. He averted his eyes, quickly grabbed the nearest doughnut, and spun around. He was already halfway up the ladder by the time Marina managed to call his name.

"Link, could we maybe ta—"

He paused midclimb, and Marina dared to hope he might come back so they could have a sit-down. Maybe even get what she hoped was their mutual attraction out in the open. But he made up for the pause with a sudden burst of speed and was gone. The coffee turned in her stomach.

She slid into the booth and prepared her little speech. At least he'd have to sit there for the study session, and

she could sneak in an apology while he was confined. But when the session began, he walked in at the last minute and did the unthinkable. He broke the code of sitting at the same table every meeting. Instead, he got cozy next to Rhee across the aisle. Marina felt sick.

As if she was reading her mind, Rhee looked up and caught Marina staring. She sidled closer to Link and leaned in to whisper something to him.

Marina stared hard at the table wishing she was diving with manta rays . . . or great whites or electric eels for that matter. Anywhere would be better than having to sit and watch that.

Simon and Kristen slid into the booth. Their table felt empty with Jeanette still up in bed sleeping off her accidental hangover. Kristen noticed Link sitting with Rhee and gave Marina a sympathetic smile. Marina held her head high and swallowed back the lump in her throat. People being sweet and sympathetic when she was upset made it even harder not to cry. She'd screwed up and hurt a friend by not being honest. She deserved to feel miserable.

Ryan sat down next to Marina as Captain Ron walked in to start the study session.

"How is she?" Ryan whispered.

"Marco gave her some extra-strength painkillers and made her drink a big glass of milk to help coat her stomach before she crashed. She was too busy dancing to eat, so she's probably gonna be pretty sick today. Marco also brought up a big jug of ice water for her to drink when she wakes up. I think he feels really bad for not noticing the telltale coconuts," Marina said.

It was kind of funny. The bartender told them that one of the little boys Jeanette was dancing with asked for a drink in a coconut for the gringa. Jeanette had asked for something islandy. Kids were always sent to bring back the drinks for their parents, so the bartender didn't think anything of it and sent back the sweet but alcohol-filled drink.

Captain Ron cleared his throat and began relaying how the whale sharks ate. Marina opened her notebook and started taking notes.

"So these guys, these gentle giants, we like to say, they dive deep and come straight up toward the surface with that big old mouth open until they hit air and then swallow the food trapped inside. They squirt the water out through these rakes they have on their gills. Food gets stuck in the rakes, and they call that dinner. They like the krill, the plankton, some small fish."

He waited a minute for all the scribbling to finish before continuing.

"Marco tells me about your TripTask program. We have room on the whale shark boats only for you in my focus groups, so I was trying to sort out what you others might do to lend a hand around the place. There's the hull scraping. Our boats get loaded with algae and barnacles and

things that slow them down. Besides wasting time better spent checking out the sharks, it costs more in fuel for the facility. Educational? I dunno. But it is a chore our biologists usually get stuck with, so you'd learn about sucking it up and getting the job done even if you have your degree," said Captain Ron.

That was the second time someone had mentioned the downside of being a marine biologist. Marina found it wasn't bothering her at all. A lot of jobs had not-so-fun parts. And at least you still got to hang out on an island while doing these.

"You can also help our two onsite marine biologists with their fish counting and coral measuring study dives. So that could be another choice."

Ryan raised his hand.

"What exactly is involved in the fish counting and coral-measuring dives?" he asked.

Captain Ron smiled. "Well, it's real complicated. First you dive with our team. And then you count fish and measure coral"—he laughed—"literally. The team shows you an identification card, and you count how many blue tang fish, or whatever species you see down under. For the coral, we have rulers with millimeter notches. You'll be visiting the coral beds we study on a regular basis to check out the health of the reef."

Ryan made a note. Marina thought that sort of task would be perfect for him.

"See, we had a bad hurricane pass through some years ago. Hurricane Mitch, back in '98. We got lucky here, compared to the other Bay Islands of Honduras. Didn't lose even one of us Utilians. But elkhorn and staghorn coral, because of their shape, got damaged—big time. We've bounced back from the hurricane, but once we had such a good record system for the area, we kept at it. Basically, now we are looking to see what effect tourism and storms and global warming have on the reef."

It was cool how Captain Ron knew so much without losing his sense of fun. He made a great teacher in that way.

"The other thing, a little more educational but not as marine-related, is that we have a team of archaeologists from an American university on the island. I talked to their director, and he said he could use a gofer to help out on their expeditions. Long days, but I think that ought to be worth some of those points. Maybe you'll find some pirate treasure. See this here tooth? Straight from Sir Francis Drake's loot. Melted it down from one of those coins he left lying all about the place," he said.

Marina noticed that, when he talked about his gold tooth, it was the first time he wasn't smiling and winking. That must mean he was joking. He turned to the side like he read her mind and gave their table a little wink the rest of the group couldn't see.

Tali raised her hand. "What exactly is a gopher? Does

that mean you dig like the animal does?" she asked.

"It's a highly technical term. See, you get on the site with them, and then when they need something, you 'go fer' this and you 'go fer' that." Captain Ron laughed. "You don't have to know too much about archaeology, just have to be able to follow orders."

"That is the perfect job for you, Tali," said Rhee, her tone innocent, but Marina thought she saw a nasty glint in the French girl's eyes.

"You think?" Tali spun around to Captain Ron with her hand raised high. "My name is Tali. I could do that."

The other students grumbled. The tasks were supposed to be listed so that everyone had a shot at signing up. But Captain Ron nodded and wrote her name on his clipboard, then continued his lecture about whale sharks. Tali and Rhee both looked pleased with themselves, but Marina had the feeling it was for two very different reasons. She wouldn't be surprised if Rhee was looking for a way to ditch her tagalong. Probably so Rhee would have more time to make a play for Link. And Marina, with her stupid lie, paved the way for her to move right in on him. She had no one to blame but herself.

Chapter Fourteen

Marina went on every dive she could during the two weeks in Utila. She really needed the distraction from the Damon and Link issues, so she and Ryan were combining the fun of diving with counting fish and measuring coral.

She always loved it, but with every dive, Marina felt more and more confident in the water. She was now able to zoom along above the coral reef and even use her breathing to float up or settle down to get a better look at the amazing fish and crustaceans.

Ryan snapped a picture of her just inches from a four-foot-long green moray eel hiding in a chunk of purple and pink coral reef. It came out so great, she was using it as her screensaver. It looked ferocious opening its mouth, full of large white needlelike teeth. Captain Ron had explained that eels opened and closed their mouths to breathe. It was only when they weren't flashing their teeth that you had to worry.

She wished she could tell Link about it, but he had been MIA lately. She didn't know where he was spending his time, but it wasn't anywhere she'd run into him. She hoped it wasn't with Rhee.

Spending several hours a day underwater was a great distraction though. Everywhere she looked she saw long yellow trumpet fish, porcupine-like puffer fish with giant blue eyes, little red-and-white-striped shrimp that would clean bigger fish by dancing across them, and lobsters the size of small dogs tucked into crevices in the reef. They even saw a squishy-looking purple barrel sponge right next to an orange elephant ear sponge. After seeing all this, she was never going to waste her time diving in cold, dark, lake water again!

Ryan was trying to collect enough photos of rare marine life to create a portfolio to enter in a big photography contest back home. He'd be up against professionals, but he hoped the uniqueness of his subjects would give him an edge. He had a list, and it was like an exciting scavenger hunt to find the animals. Marina thought he looked like a different person when he was talking about his pictures.

He just came alive. He kind of looked that way when he was talking with Jeanette, too, she realized.

One afternoon, as Marina and Ryan were on the boat heading back to the dock, Ryan rattled on about the shots he'd snapped of two tiny seahorses that blended in so well on the sea wall that even a foot away it was easy to miss them. Unfortunately, not so easy for Marina to miss was the sight of Link, walking down the beach with a beautiful local girl.

"Who's that?" Marina asked before she could stop herself.

Ryan turned and looked uneasy at the sight. "I dunno. Let's go grab a soda," he said, changing the subject.

Marina let herself be pulled away from the rail. Jeanette always knew everything going on on the boat; maybe she'd know what was up with Link.

That night, when they were lying in their bunks, Marina brought it up. "So, guess what," she began.

"What?" Jeanette asked. She was typing another letter to her dad. "Wait. Do you think I could just put three-to-five-foot shark instead of thirty-to-fifty-foot? I mean, what's a few zeros here and there? Could be a typo, right?"

Marina laughed. "I saw Link walking on the beach today with a beyond gorgeous local girl with the prettiest dark ebony skin, long tiny braids, and—" Marina started.

"A killer bod?" Jeanette finished.

Marina sighed and stared at the wood slats of the bunk

above her. "Yeah, that's sounds about right," she admitted.

"Don't know who she is. Link's been with her since a few days after we got here. She picks him up right after you guys head out on your morning dive, and they come back right before you guys come in from the afternoon dive."

That explained why Link was never around for lunch. Oh, well. It wasn't any of her business, anyway. She rolled over and hugged Dude tight, until she remembered he was Damon's gift to remember *him* by.

Marina was usually back on the boat in time to see Tali come home each day dripping with sweat from her long walks through town on the sweltering concrete streets. Rumor had it that the head of the dig was so impressed with her mathematical abilities and grasp of the scientific details that he let her join in when not running errands. After ten days elbow deep in sandy dirt, Tali had found six shards of pottery from some aboriginal Indians. She was thrilled and showed off the Polaroids of her find to anyone who would look. Marina was glad Tali had found her niche. Marina told Jeanette about it that afternoon.

"I'm so jealous. Can you imagine? Touching something that ancient? The Indians sat right here on the island where we are, cooking or whatever with those exact pots! I felt really bad for Tali, though. She was all excited about her artifacts and she rushed to show Rhee the pictures."

"Uh-oh, What'd Rhee say?" Jeanette asked.

Marina handed up a bottle of Coke. "Nothing really. Luckily Tali seemed to miss the fact that Rhee was decidedly unimpressed with her find."

"Speaking of unimpressed, the locals aren't diggin' Rhee's little habit of sunbathing topless like she did at home."

"Ooooh. Did they say something?"

"Of course. I mean, the girl lays on the top deck half naked just about every afternoon in plain view of that really conservative church down the beach! I heard the pastor complained to Marco directly, and Marco docked Rhee most of her TripTask points for disregarding local customs."

"Oh my *God*! No way!"

"Yep. So it looks like there's one less competitor for the big dive trip."

They giggled and passed a bag of fried plantain chips back and forth. Marina hadn't known what she'd been missing by lacking a girlfriend to gossip with back home.

Even with the ongoing Damon and Link problems hanging over her head, Marina was enjoying the island so much, she was sad to see the last morning arrive. She had felt the same way when it was time to leave the Bahamas, though,

and once she stopped dwelling on the past, another great adventure had popped up that almost equaled it. That seemed to be the way the world worked.

She was heading down for their last breakfast when she stopped short. That was it. She just needed to let go. She was holding not only herself back from whatever great new experiences were to come, but Damon, too. And he didn't even know it. It suddenly seemed really unfair of her. There would never be a perfect time to say good-bye, especially considering his mom's illness. But knowing there was no future for them, she owed it to Damon to let him be free to see what life brought his way. She ran back to the cabin and pulled out her laptop before she lost her nerve.

From: Marinabiology@email.com
To: SkierBoi@email.com
Subject: Us

Damon,

You have meant so much to me and I have grown so much in our time together. I think that is actually the problem. We have both grown, and sometimes you just don't grow together, you know? I think we are going in different directions. I know this time apart has been tough on both of us. I am sorry if I have hurt you by going away. It was just something I needed to do. I know now that I can't make you happy, that I can't be happy myself, following the path we thought we'd take together. We want different things, and I admire you for wanting to stay close to home. I know even though your mom is in remission, it will mean a lot to your family to have you nearby. And you have a whole life with the ski team that I'm not really a part of. I guess I am saying that trying to ignore that, and pretending we don't mind giving up the things we love will only make us resent each other. You are my best friend and have been from the beginning of "us." That makes this so much harder. Because you don't stop loving your best friend.

I hate doing this over e-mail, but being honest is so important, even when it is really hard. I just felt that it couldn't wait.

Love, Marina

Marina let the tears slide down over her cheeks as she read her words. It was okay to hurt. It was her past she was letting go of. It needed to be done, but her finger still hovered over the keyboard for a long time. She took a deep breath, closed her eyes, and hit send.

On the way to the dining room, she stood for a minute at the deck rail, letting the comforting sound of the sea breeze rustling the palm tree fronds wash over her.

"You look different," Jeanette said as Marina finally walked up to the table.

"I feel different," Marina said, without explaining.

Link didn't respond. After the first day of avoiding Marina, he had returned to their table. He usually ate then ran off after the study session to wherever he went with the local girl.

Captain Ron wandered in without his clipboard as the others sat down. Marina set her mind back on the trip. She couldn't help it when she missed the last day in the Bahamas. But she wasn't going to mope around and miss out on the last day in Utila.

"Hello, all. Don't worry, I'm a few minutes early today. Just wanted to thank you. You've done a great job here. We are set for coral and fish data, and our boats will be gliding along that sea. Never seen such a scraping! And your classmates on the focus teams helped us find and tag four new animals, which might be a record for us here!"

Everyone clapped. Simon hugged a proud Kristen.

"And I had the best time working with the archaeology team," Tali piped up. "Thank you for the opportunity!" She was still clutching her Polaroids everywhere she went.

"But you did not find a thing related to pirates on the dig," Rhee said.

Captain Ron looked at Rhee and laughed.

"Well, I'm not too surprised about that. After all, the only real find on Utila was when they found a gold, jeweled cup in a cave by Pumpkin Hill. And don't tell anyone, but my primo, Jessie, said he heard that came from some church over there on the mainland. But I'm glad you enjoyed your time so much, Tali. I heard equally good things about you from the team, so I've asked Marco to add some extra TripTask points to your total. They said you were much less loafer and far more gofer than they usually end up with."

Marina had to smile at the shock on Rhee's face.

"So I know the rest of you been disappointed about those whale shark boats all being full every day. And I know you don't really want to go all the way to Australia to see one of them whale sharks for yourselves. So I was thinking…"

He paused with a mischievous smile.

"Maybe you'd like to have a private whale shark cruise with the best captain in the business?"

They cheered, and Marina's heart sped up. It was thrilling to think of, but kind of scary, too. Knowing the sharks would be bigger than the boat was enough to make her nervous, despite loving everything she'd seen underwater so far. She could always go on the trip and watch the sharks from the boat, though. Just because the others went in the ocean with the sharks didn't mean she had to.

"So, no class this morning. Enjoy your last day. Go into town or go out on the boats for a dive. Enjoy yourselves, and we'll see you back at the dock by five for your whale shark cruise before you head off to the Dominican Republic."

They watched him swagger back out.

"Hey, Tali? Wanna go to town and shop for souvenirs?" Teresa called.

Tali looked uncertainly at Rhee and then back to Teresa.

"She must want you to go and calculate the exchange rate from Honduran lempira to U.S. dollars for her," Rhee said. "Come on, Tali, let's go up and lay out." Rhee turned to Teresa with a sneer, "It's fourteen to one, Teresa. Not that difficult: fourteen, twenty-eight, forty-two, fifty-eight—"

"Um, actually Rhee, that's fifty-six, not fifty-eight. And I kind of wanted to get something for my mom. Thanks for inviting me, Teresa."

Tali hurried out of the dining area, leaving a stunned Rhee behind. Marina stifled her giggle.

"Anyone up for a dive?" Ryan asked.

"I am, for sure!" Marina said.

"Count me in," said Jeanette.

"It's our focus group's last morning trip, but we'll see you guys on the cruise this afternoon," Simon explained.

"You guys mind if I join you?" Link asked.

Marina almost choked on her coffee. She went back over the conversation in her head, but she was sure she'd already said she was going on the dive. Maybe Link was finally starting to warm up again. Or maybe he was so into that local girl that a little misunderstanding with Marina meant nothing. It wasn't like they were going out or anything.

Ryan seemed to read her mind.

"Great. But what about—" he stopped abruptly.

"I've said my good-byes there," Link said quietly.

Marina decided not to analyze it any more. They were just four friends about to spend the morning the best way possible—diving. How and why didn't matter.

After their morning dive, Marina patted an upset Jeanette on the shoulder. They sat waiting for their tanks to be switched to new ones for the second dive. Jeanette had spent the first dive struggling to stay at a level depth in the water. Ryan had really stepped up to help. He held her hand and pulled her along, but Marina could see the frustration on Jeanette's face.

"Been thinking. It must be your weights. They were probably off. Gotta be," Link said.

"I don't see how. Everyone else's were fine, and I haven't had problems with my weights on other dives," said Jeanette.

"But this equipment is different. Look, some people are floaters; some people are sinkers—I think you're a floater. You have too little on your weight belt. It makes it hard to get down and stay there," Link explained.

"But I've got less weights than Jeanette, and I'm way bigger," Marina said.

"Yeah, but she's got a lot more body fat," Ryan said.

Jeanette's mouth dropped open, and she swung her

flippers at him. "Hey! What the hell is your problem?"

"I didn't mean... I mean, it's not a bad thing. You have your body fat in good places to have body fat. I was just saying. I mean, Marina's pretty fl— er, just doesn't have those sort of chunks or, well, her body is more on the slim side, um, like streamlined? And yours is, look, I was just trying—"

Ryan looked in desperation at Link, who was shaking his head and laughing while putting as much distance as possible between them on the small boat.

"You are so on your own, man," Link said.

"Why don't you keep your eyes on your lenses and off our bodies, Photoboy," spat Jeanette.

She glared at him with a ferocity that made him flinch. Marina wanted to be offended by the "flat" comment, but Ryan's bumbling cluelessness made her smile.

"Come on, Jeanette, let's go check your weights again. And after I've done that, I'll teach Ryan here how to talk to a girl," said Link.

With his usual miserable expression, Ryan watched them switching around weights on the front of the boat. Marina sat next to him.

"Ryan?"

"What."

"You just gotta tell her."

"Tell her what?"

"That you're into her."

"Yeah, right. She hates me!"

He motioned with his chin toward Jeanette, who was throwing him dagger looks. Marina swallowed a giggle.

"Look, I know it seems that way. But I think she likes you. If she hated you as much as it seems, why would she keep spending all her time with you? People just show their feelings in different ways. She's used to guys like Link, or the guys at that band dance," Marina said.

"Great," Ryan said.

"No. I just mean, you know, guys who are really forward. So take a chance, see what happens. Don't miss out on these last few weeks!"

Ryan looked down at his fins and nodded.

Late that afternoon, Marina sat on the back deck of the whale shark speedboat by herself and played with her snorkel mask. Maybe it was the breakup e-mail affecting her mood, but she really didn't want to get in the water. She wished you could dive, instead of snorkel, with whale sharks, but they came up only for short periods of time to feed. Otherwise, they were so deep it would be impossible to catch sight of one. She felt much more secure wearing her tank and dive gear underwater than floating on the surface.

Ryan had just come and pulled Jeanette away. They were talking quietly on the other side of the boat.

Link approached Marina and leaned on the ledge next

to her. They settled into the same companionable silence they shared on the night of the BabyWatch. It seemed like so much longer than two weeks had passed.

Jeanette was holding something small in her hands and started jumping up and down and hugging Ryan. Marina laughed.

"I guess he had a grand gesture in him after all," she said.

Jeanette ran over to Marina.

"Look! Look what he got me!"

"What is it?" Marina asked.

Jeanette showed her a little silver turtle. It hung from a single ring.

"It's a belly ring! From the Bahamas. He had them make it way back in the Bahamas!" Jeanette said.

Ryan walked over and looked up sheepishly.

"Nice one, Ryan!" Link said.

"A belly ring? But I thought you said—" Marina started.

"Well, I guess self-mutilation just looks better on some people than others," Ryan said.

He grabbed a beaming Jeanette's hand. Over their shoulders, Marina noticed a huge flock of seabirds circling and diving. The boat lurched as Captain Ron turned the vessel around and yelled for them all to get their masks on and line up at the back of the boat.

She stood up in surprise as she saw the group heading

their way. Ryan and Jeanette ran for their snorkel gear. The water ahead looked like it was bubbling, and Marina decided there was no way she was going in. Without her dive gear on, she felt as protected as if she were wearing nothing at all.

"You guys go ahead, I'm gonna stay on board for this—" Marina called to the jostling group trying to peer around her at the sea.

Rhee had managed to elbow her way to the front. She looked behind her and grabbed Marina's arm.

"Are you making a joke? This is a whale shark. You will be missing out on a once-in-a-lifetime chance."

Marina was shocked. Was it possible that Rhee was actually being thoughtful? Maybe Rhee just hoped the giant shark would eat Marina. Or maybe the little scene earlier with Tali made Rhee rethink her attitude.

Captain Ron pointed directly behind the boat. From his perch up in the captain's tower he had the ability to see right through the crystal water.

"Whale shark!"

Marina decided to let them all pass and then decide whether to go in. She was edging her way to the side of the group when she felt Rhee's shoulder push against her.

"You will thank me for this later," said Rhee.

Marina caught sight of her own flipper flying over her head as she landed upside down, headfirst in the sea.

Luckily, her weeks of diving had paid off. Marina spun easily around in a somersault and kicked to the surface. It wasn't until she saw the distinctive white spots and stripes under her that she realized she was directly above a humongous whale shark. Her fear slipped away as she recognized its grace and beauty. It was gliding along a few feet under the water, swimming slowly, totally relaxed. Marina noticed a tiny tag in its top dorsal fin and wondered if it was one the crew had tagged earlier that week. She looked behind her and saw that most of the students were kicking along the length of the creature.

Link free dove down to touch its brown skin, then kicked his way up near Marina. The shark was so long that six or seven students fit easily along its body on each side. It didn't seem to mind the attention. It was supposed to have the thickest skin of any animal, so maybe it didn't even feel them through four inches of the stuff. Just in case, she folded her arms together so she wouldn't accidentally startle it with her touch. She took a deep breath and went under, using the long steady strokes she'd perfected in her many dives.

Marina looked across the broad flat back of the whale shark's body and gently touched its side. She drew her hand back at the surprising coarse sandpaper texture. It looked so smooth!

The shark must have been five or six feet wide. There were several sharklike remora fish no more than a foot or so long attached to the underside of the whale shark. They slid around but stayed suckered on by their mouths—parasites waiting for a free meal. Rhee was on the other side flailing around and trying to stay upright while fiddling to get water out of her snorkel mask.

Marina ignored her and kicked farther up and over the checked pattern of stripes and spots across the whale shark's three back ridges to inspect the small eye on the side of its head. She laughed out loud in delight, sending a plume of water shooting out of her snorkel tube. She was underwater. In the Caribbean. Looking into the eye of the biggest fish in the world! She grabbed Link's passing hand and squeezed it. She just had to share the high of the experience. His mouth grinned around the snorkel mouthpiece, and together they kicked up the length of the shark. Her body was tingling from snorkel tube to fin tip.

The shark slowed, and Marina and Link passed by its head. Marina turned to enjoy the view from the front and cringed. Rhee was awkwardly struggling on the surface, apparently having sucked some water through her snorkel tube. Her flipper smacked into the shark as she kicked wildly. The whale shark flinched and jerked toward Marina. Before she knew it, she was staring into the five-foot-wide open mouth of a whale shark!

Marina gasped and sucked in a bit of water herself as she realized it really could swallow her whole. The shark moved forward, and, as she held her breath, it closed its

mouth and dipped its head, diving down just below her. Marina felt Link take her hand and pull her to the surface. She watched as, with one big whoosh of its tail fin, the shark zoomed straight down and disappeared.

She gasped for breath when she reached the surface, and it hit her that she had just swam with her first shark. A very big first shark. She clung to Link and tried to wrap her mind around the pure terror and joy that mingled together to make her heart thud so hard she figured she could see her chest thumping in and out. She even looked down to check. The sight of Link pressed so close made her heart speed up a notch more. The students were whooping and hollering in exhilaration on the surface. Captain Ron stood up on the captain's tower silhouetted by the setting sun. He nodded down at them and grabbed the air horn to add to the racket.

They stayed in the water celebrating the end of their stay in Utila for several minutes before heading back to the boat. Marina was surprised and thrilled that Link didn't let go of her until nearly all the students were back on board. She tried to compose herself as they swam back toward the back deck, but even the realization that she owed Rhee a huge thank-you couldn't wipe the grin off her face.

Chapter Fifteen

The trip from Utila to the Dominican Republic was their longest voyage yet, but the high from the whale shark experience the day before kept everyone in good spirits. Marina had tried to thank Rhee, but the French girl claimed that she just didn't feel like listening to Marina whine because she'd missed the experience. Marina decided that Rhee was only 99 percent evil. Maybe even just 98 percent.

After lunch, Marina's tablemates and a few other students decided to hang out in the lounge and watch some of Ryan's underwater shots from the Utila dives. Marina

and Link sat on the sofa next to Ryan. Jeanette sat on the carpeted floor between Ryan's knees.

Through Ryan kept offering his disclaimer that putting together digital slide shows on a computer wasn't his specialty, the images seamlessly morphed into each other with background music cues. Ryan just had an eye for the perfect shot. He also had an eye for a certain curly-haired, freckled fish. Marina watched Jeanette's smile grow as she noticed nearly eight of the first twenty minutes of the slideshow images were of her.

"Wasn't there anything else to photograph?" Rhee said.

"Oh, hey! What a shock! It's Jeanette again!" Link teased.

Ryan threw a pillow past Marina at Link. Some of the other students joined them in the room when they had finished their lunch. Tali was seasick again. But with Marco's hints and some of Simon's candied ginger, at least she was able to join the rest of them in the lounge. She slid to the floor onto a huge pillow.

Kristen leaned in toward the screen. "That reef looks amazing!"

"Oh, that's right. You didn't get much chance to dive, being on the whale shark boats, did you?" Marina said.

"What a bummer!" said Jeanette.

Simon shrugged. "Well, we did some diving in the Bahamas."

"Really?" asked Marina.

"We got onto six different dolphin dives, in between all that data entry about the different dolphin species," Kristen answered.

"We're hoping to win the incentive prize so that we can have another week together." Simon pulled Kris in for a hug. "Maybe next Christmas, if we can talk our parents into it."

"Everyone's been trying hard." Jeanette shrieked and playfully swatted Ryan as a close-up of her backside filled the screen. "It'll be interesting to see who comes away with the trip. It must be pretty even with the points."

"Except for Marina. Remember the baby dolphin? That was so cool. She'll get it for sure!" said Tali.

Rhee snorted and gave Tali a look.

Ryan got up to open the second slide-show file. Everyone clapped as the whale shark came onto the screen.

Marina focused on the photos until she felt her leg brush up against Link's. She started to move it when he looked at her with a distracted smile. He'd been really quiet since they left Utila. Marina wondered if he missed the girl from the beach. That reminded her that she hadn't checked her e-mail for word from Damon today. She'd been checking regularly since she sent the breakup e-mail. She excused herself and headed up to the cabin.

She looked out the porthole while the laptop powered

up. The sea was a darker blue this far from land. She wondered if any whale sharks wandered out this far.

She heard the familiar whooshing sign of new mail and held her breath. There was one from Damon. With no subject. It was always bad when an e-mail came with no subject. She clicked on the message with a bittersweet combination of dread and anticipation.

From: SkierBoi@email.com
To: Marinabiology@email.com
Subject: [no subject]

Marina,

Wow. Okay. God, this sucks. I was expecting this. Kind of for a while now. Maybe even before you left. But it still sucks. I guess you're right. This is my home up here. It's where I need to be. When we started out, running off to Hawaii sounded like a good time. But the stuff with my mom happened, and having a good time kind of isn't my first priority anymore. But you were there for me through all that, and I didn't want to let you down. So I get it—you gotta be where you need to be, and I gotta be where I need to be. I wish it was the same place. I guess I don't know what else to say. I'm bummed. Way bummed. But it's cool. You go do your thing, Marina. Good luck and all that, 'kay?

Da

Marina held her breath as she reread the e-mail. The "I didn't want to let you down" line choked her with a sob. After everything that Damon had been through in the past year, and after she'd left him alone to study abroad, he was still worried about how *she* would feel. But he hadn't let her down, and she hadn't let him down. They just weren't meant to be.

She wiped her tears away, swallowing hard, and read through the message a third time. "It's cool. You go do your thing, Marina." That was just so Damon. She couldn't help but laugh through her tears. So that was it; they were over. She tried out his line to the cabin, "It's cool." She laughed again and grabbed a tissue to blow her nose. It was going to be okay. Marina stood up and stared at the ocean, trying to recapture her calm. The rise and fall of the water always soothed her. As she swiped at her wet cheeks with a tissue, something in the water caught her eye.

Dolphins!

There were at least a hundred dolphins, and they were jumping and spinning right off the side of the boat. If that wasn't a sign that she'd done the right thing about Damon, she didn't know what was. She watched them surf the wake of the boat, and then she headed downstairs to tell the others. She would thank the gods of the seas later for sending her such an uplifting sight to sweep away her sad mood. She stuck her head into the lounge. "Dolphins! There are dolphins outside!"

Most of the students ran for the deck. Link flipped closed the magazine he was reading and stood to head outside.

"We should tell Ryan about the dolphins. He'll want to get photos," Link said.

"Where is he?"

"He went up with Jeanette to our cabin. They just left a minute ago."

"Okay, I'll go let them know. Thanks!" Marina called over her shoulder as she headed upstairs.

Ryan answered Marina's first knock. She stepped into the cabin and waved to Jeanette, who was flipping through a photo album.

"There is a huge pod of dolphins on the other side of the boat. I think they might be spinner dolphins. They look smaller than the ones we worked with," she said.

"Very cool!" Ryan immediately began gathering his photography equipment.

"Quick, Ry, can I hold anything?" Jeanette asked.

Marina looked around the cabin while he scrambled for his lenses. The guys were actually pretty neat. She was surprised. She picked up a ceramic painted vase and turned it over, checking out the sea animal pattern carved across it. As she was setting it down, she noticed writing on the bottom: *Link, Thanks for Everything! Mariposa*

She nearly dropped the thing. Mariposa. Must be his

girlfriend from Utila. She looked up and saw that Ryan had been talking to her.

"Sorry, what?" she asked.

"I asked if spinners were the ones who did all the fancy moves—the flips, the twists, and all of those? I don't know if I should bring flash or slow shot," he said, pulling out lenses and checking batteries.

Marina sat down on the lower bunk and then hopped up at the thought that it might be Link's. That just felt sort of weird.

"Yep, spinning and jumping. There's tons of them," she said.

Ryan loaded Jeanette's arms with camera equipment, and they headed to watch the wild dolphins. Link was standing at one of the rails when they got to the back deck. He pointed down at a mother and baby jumping in the swells. The baby was only a few feet long, half the size of the animals they worked with in the Bahamas, but it was doing complicated spins and jumps in the wake of the boat.

"Remind you of anyone?" Link yelled over the boat motor.

"I wonder how Gracie's baby is doing," Marina yelled back.

They moved aside so Ryan could take photos of the baby. Luckily, he had the camera in a Plexiglas underwater

housing that kept the sensitive device dry. The rest of them were getting soaked in the salty spray from the boat hitting the swells at its high cruising speed. They could see land in the far distance, and the masts of other boats in the area stood out on the blue sea.

Marina could have watched the dolphins all day and been perfectly happy, but the dive bell called them all down for a meeting. They filed into the dining room, where Marco positively bounced.

"I'm glad you all got to see the beauty of the dolphins in the wild to add to your marine experiences. We will be entering the port area of our final destination in about twenty minutes. I'd like to welcome you all to the outlying waters of my country! Yes, for those of you who didn't know, I was born and raised right here in the Dominican Republic!"

Marco's excitement was contagious, and it took a few moments for them to settle down.

"That's right, the Dominican Republic. My country covers nearly two-thirds of the island of Hispaniola, with the western third belonging to Haiti. We, like most of the Caribbean islands, have a varied peoples, descending from Europeans, Africans, and a native Indian tribe, the Tainos. These Indians left behind many cultural offerings, including the cave paintings you will see in promotions for the island as well as in some of the arts and cultural museums."

Marco opened a folder and handed out brochures for some local sites.

"The country has beautiful beaches, which is what we are most concerned with for our purposes. No, sorry, not for adding to your tans. But for the primary reason we are here—besides my sneaking in a visit with *mi madre*—the sea turtles. Leatherback, green, hawksbill, and loggerhead sea turtles all make their nests on the beaches of this country."

Jeanette and Ryan passed along the brochures to Marina. Link slid closer to read them over her shoulder.

"The project we focus on here is one that is dear to my heart. The plight of the sea turtle is dire, with some of their numbers dropping drastically. Part of the reason for this is the interference of humans on the animals' habitat. Much of the initial research will be done in the turtle refuge facility, monitoring baby turtles in various stages of development in saltwater tanks."

"Will this be like Utila, where only the focus group works with the facility?" asked Marina.

"Yes and no. Toward the end of our stay, we will need several volunteers for night shifts to patrol one of the egg-laying beaches. You'll once again have the opportunity to earn TripTask points, but not necessarily in projects that directly involve marine life. I will remind you, as your past instructors did, that this is all part of being a marine biologist—particularly when you are in an internship position.

"We are building a brand-new sea turtle refuge center here, and there will be tasks involving building the facility itself. There will be rooms for biologists and volunteers, as well as an outdoor incubation area for transplanting eggs that were laid in locations where the survival of the babies might be threated."

There were murmurs as people discussed their preferred tasks.

"Recent property development in one particular beach area is causing a need to relocate these eggs to a more suitable home where they can safely hatch. Fortunately, the turtles most often frequenting this beach are of the loggerhead variety. This is a good thing because, unlike many other species of sea turtle, the loggerhead are migratory and do not need to return to the specific beach where they themselves were born in order to lay their eggs. So, in other words, this disturbance will not affect future generations."

Rhee raised her hand. "Does this mean we will not be allowed on the beach?"

"Well, the beach where we will transplant the eggs is off limits for recreational use. Actually, it looks like we are docking up right now in the port in Samana, where you'll find several suitable beaches to enjoy. I should add, the reason I am offering this talk in such detail is that, for the most part, I will be your liaison for this project. It is a very busy time of year for the facility; most of the species of turtles they are trying to help and protect nest and lay their eggs between March and May, with varying times for hatching within that season as well. Working with the turtles here was my job while growing up and during the summers between my years in university. So in other words, you're stuck with me." Marco laughed.

The clank of the chains and ropes securing the boat was almost drowned out by an outside roar of cheers and applause. With a nod from Marco, the students wandered out on the deck to check it out. There must have been thirty people on the dock cheering.

"Friendly people here!" Link yelled to Marco.

The people parted to allow an older Dominican woman to move to the front. Marco blew her a kiss and yelled above the din.

"Family always is!"

Chapter Sixteen

Marina and Link settled into an uneasy friendship as their roommates got swept away from them and into their focus project. Actually, it wasn't so much *un*easy as *too* easy. They just couldn't seem to spend time together without things building toward something more than friendship. Link didn't seem to mind, but Marina didn't want to be a rebound girl for him. It would be better to have a place as a good friend than just some fling to take his mind off the beautiful island girl. So when flirtations arose, Marina kept a handle on things by reciting "Mariposa, Mariposa, Mariposa" in her head to kill the mood.

Also killing the mood were the morning study sessions about turtles. Marina couldn't believe some of the awful things that people did to profit from sea turtles. She'd learned to eat her breakfast before Marco began his study sessions. His normal wide smile disappeared as he recounted some of the abuses inflicted on the gentle animals.

"In our lectures we've covered the leatherbacks, the green sea turtles, and the loggerheads, whose eggs we'll be working with at the facility. Today we'll be talking about the hawksbill turtle. The hawksbill turtle is found in the Cabo Rojo region of beaches in our country. With the distinctive overlapping shingled effect to its shell, its greatest decline in numbers, sadly, is due to the hunting and selling of the shell for art. Their shell can bring more than one hundred dollars per pound. Their skin is also used in leather products, and their skin's oil can be found in perfumes and makeup. It doesn't matter that they are labeled 'endangered.' These animals are harvested for money."

Marina looked around. Everyone else seemed as glum as she did.

"I know this is hard to handle. But we have to be realists and understand what we are up against in order to plan for and address the issues. Some of these may seem impossible to combat, such as the hawksbills being killed for art and vanity products. But as we raise awareness and stop people from buying them, the price will go down as

the demand decreases. Eventually, we will see a rise in the turtles' numbers."

Marco wrapped up his talk, and everyone filed out quietly. Link had invited Marina to the Samana beach for the day, so they put away their notebooks and headed out. As they walked through the colorful market, Link grabbed her hand and pulled her to a stall to show her an engraved shell. When they left the booth, he didn't let go. Marina's stomach fluttered at the gesture, but now that she and Damon were officially over, she figured it was okay to relax her ground rules a bit. Walking through the market hand in hand didn't feel like a big deal. It was natural and easy.

Far from Link's initial sexist attitude, he'd been respect-ful and thoughtful on their outings. She hadn't missed the fact that his eyes never wandered to any of the many gor-geous island girls checking him out.

Link pulled her up to an artisan's stall full of carnival masks. The owner came right over.

"Carnival masks," the older man said.

Marina was grateful he spoke English. Although Spanish was the official language here, Marco had said most of the people working with tourists spoke at least a little bit of English.

"What do they mean?" Link asked.

"All different regions celebrate in different style," the man explained.

Link pointed to a large mask with a crisscross blue-

and-red ribbon design on the face and huge cowlike horns covered with purple and pink flowers. Carnival had ended just three weeks before they arrived, and, looking at the bizarre masks, Marina was sorry they'd missed it.

Link picked up a mask.

Seeing his interest, the man went into sales-pitch mode. "Good quality. Horns, skins, hooves—all real. Clay for the face, the rest from the slaughterhouse for the mask."

Marina set down the mask she held. She had almost tried it on, which was too gross even to think about. Link would never kiss her if she had dead cow hooves hanging from her head. She caught herself and blushed.

Marina acknowledged to herself that she'd had a fantasy run through her head approximately every eleven seconds of Link and her on the Galápagos *Tiburon* together. Now she was adding to her daydreams thoughts of his kissing her in the middle of the market. Reminding herself of Mariposa wasn't going to be enough to squash this. And besides, Link had been holding *her* hand today, not Mariposa's. She sighed.

"What's the matter?" Link asked.

"Nothing. It's just, I need to talk to you about something before I lose my mind entirely," she said.

"Is this a good something or a bad something?"

"Well, I'm not sure." She saw a sign for LA PLAYA at the far end of the market. She thanked the man and pulled Link toward the beach.

Marina sat down with Link in two chaise lounge rentals under a shady palm on the beach. They paid the chair guy, and Link stared at her while she tried to think of where to begin.

She turned toward him and then looked away again. They sat in their individual chaise lounges separated by two feet of beach and one big lie. When she started to apologize, he looked in her eyes.

"So I just, well, wasn't sure about things, and I was scared. I wasn't lying on purpose. It didn't start out like that at least. I just didn't ever want to hurt you, or maybe you weren't hurt—maybe you were just mad? Sorry. I'm not making sense," she mumbled.

Link finally looked away. He stared at the shoreline for a long minute before taking her hands in his and looking back into her face.

"You know what doesn't make sense?"

Marina held his gaze and her breath.

"What?" she managed.

Link tugged on her braid and smiled his crooked smile.

"That we let all this stupid stuff keep us apart during the last two weeks in Utila."

He pulled her over toward his chaise lounge. His hand slid up to her cheek, and their lips met in the middle of the two chairs. It was a long, slow kiss. Marina was so caught by surprise she found herself staring at the lashes of his closed eyes. Finally, she closed her eyes too, and let herself drift into it. With Link's strong hand on her back, the sand beneath her feet, and the warm breeze lifting her hair away from her face—it was most definitely the best kiss of her life.

Chapter Seventeen

Once it was clear they had something special, Marina and Link had put all efforts into the TripTask points. Making the Galápagos fantasy a reality was worth spending the remaining days working instead of lounging on the beach.

"Hey, Marina. The facility is taking us out on a dive to see turtles in their natural environment. There are two extra spots. Do you and Link want to come?" Ryan asked.

"Definitely!"

"Grab your stuff. Marco is coming for us in about twenty minutes."

"Cool!"

Marina smiled as she ran to tell Link. She knew he'd want to come. The hours spent in the turtle refuge center had brought them even closer. It was all positive energy there. Rhee had given up on winning the free trip after being docked points for her topless sunbathing in Utila, so she was conveniently out of everyone's hair at the facility. Even the dreaded study sessions about how bad things were going for some turtle species were easier to handle when you spent the day creating a habitat for baby turtles.

Marina found Link in his room and quickly helped him gather his stuff. Just as she thought, he was excited to go on this dive. They headed out to the boat, hand in hand, and found Marco waiting.

The boat they took out to the dive spot wasn't much bigger than a skiff. And, without a dock, they'd have to use the navy-seal-like backward flip method of entering the ocean instead of the usual giant step out. The engine threw a rooster tail of water behind them as they zoomed over the crystal clear turquoise waters. The coral reef below passed by in a blur of oranges and purples. This area of the island was frequented by locals, and the boat driver raised a lazy hand to some friends on the palm tree–covered beach. As the boat slowed down, Marco's expression darkened.

A small red, green, and yellow boat was anchored to the reef. Marco nodded to the driver, who shook his head

and revved the engine a few times. The young teen who was napping in the boat jumped up and banged the side of the boat with a wrench.

"What's going on?" asked Ryan.

"Poachers, looks like. It's bad enough they are dropping anchor and destroying the coral and sponges below. But you can bet they aren't just out here for a scenic dive."

"How can they do that? Isn't it protected by laws?" Marina asked.

"Not all of the reef system. This area is a well-known turtle-cleaning station. We've been trying to widen the marine reserve to include it, but paperwork moves slowly here," said Marco.

"What's a cleaning station?" asked Jeanette.

"It's an area rich in cleaner shrimp and tiny cleaning fish. The turtles come to have the bacteria and parasites removed from their shells. And the cleaner shrimp and fish survive on the algae and bits of food they take off the turtles. It's a perfect example of the kind of symbiotic relationship that makes the undersea world so efficient."

They watched as two divers came up to the colorful boat and handed net bags to the teen. They were too far away to make out their faces, but the teen yelled something to the divers, who then scrambled up into the boat as he started the engine. The outboard motor whined as he reversed and they yanked the anchor from the reef with a loud scrape. The front of the boat rose in the air as they put the throttle on and headed toward a small rickety dock in the distance. Marco watched them go with sad eyes.

"The turtles all know to come to this spot. The problem is, so do the poachers."

"Were those turtles in the bags? What will they do with them? They're not going to kill them, are they?" Jeanette asked.

"Maybe. Maybe not. Another method of profiting from the creatures is selling and reselling live turtles. Kids make a quick buck hitting up an ecological-minded tourist for a bribe to let the turtles go. They even give the turtle to the tourist to release. It's no solution. They release them from the beach there, and the turtles come right back out here. And so do the poachers. Only this time, there are even more poachers because their friends hear how easy the money is."

"That's just so wrong," said Marina.

"It's heartbreaking. At first they tried to sell them to the facility, but we wouldn't stand for it. Sure, there is a cleaning station in the protected area closer to where the *Tiburon* is docked, but relocating an entire population of turtles is impossible. If the elders knew what some of these teens were doing to get their disco and beer money, they'd put an end to it and quick. But tourists don't know one local from another, and there are a lot of good kids who shouldn't have to pay for the misdeeds of others."

They were all quiet as they readied their gear for the

dive. As they dropped down through the water, Marco pointed out a large gash of smashed and broken coral left behind by the poachers' anchor.

A turtle almost as long as Marina glided down. It rested on its stomach on the white sand near the edge of the reef. Within seconds, five or six red-and-white-striped shrimp ran out and crawled all over its back. Tiny purple and yellow fish poked at the shell, nibbling off bits of algae. Marina was amazed to see the shrimp crawl right onto the turtle's face with busy legs and antenna running over its eyelids to remove dead skin and bacteria. After a few minutes, the shrimp and fish scooted back to their crevices in the coral, and the large turtle swam away. The cleaning station reminded Marina of an underwater car wash.

Link grabbed her hand and pointed up. There were three other turtles swimming in lazy circles like planes waiting to land. They observed the cleaning operation, occasionally tipping their heads up to take a breath. As soon as the first turtle vacated the spot, a new turtle swooped down for its turn.

It was an amazing sight, but one that left the group near speechless on the trip back to the dock. Because as thrilling as it was to see a turtle-cleaning station, the sight of the poaching boat marred the memory of the experience.

Chapter Eighteen

Marina and Link were sitting in their booth on the boat, their legs resting against each other while they sipped their coffees. It was how they'd spent every minute since the day of their first kiss—as close as possible.

Ryan and Jeanette would be sleeping half the day after pulling an all-night shift relocating the turtle eggs. They were burying them in the same sandy spot Marina and Link had covered with chicken wire the day before to protect the eggs from predators.

Marco walked by as Kris and Simon slid into their booth. "What are you doing sitting inside on a beautiful day. You

should hit the beach. I need you guys to collect coconuts for the good-bye party tomorrow. My mother is going to make you a local dish—Pescado Con Coco—cooked over an open fire. Look for the brown husked coconuts. Knock on them. If they sound hollow, they are good to go. Green ones will be full of Jell-O–like pulp. We need the hard meat ones. There are plenty of palms to check under."

Marina and Link joined the large group on the beach and managed to find ten good coconuts for Marco's stew. They had taken a minibus out of town a bit to a beach near the turtle refuge. No sense in searching for coconuts where everyone else in the city would be.

Ryan and Jeanette walked ahead holding hands. Marina smiled and reached out to take Link's hand. He smiled his lazy smile.

"Guys?"

Something in Simon's tone made Link's smile fall, and Marina looked to where Simon was motioning. There were three teenagers sitting in the sand holding a large burlap bag. They eyed the group from the brush. Marina felt prickles go up her spine. There was something about the situation that didn't feel right.

"*Disculpa, senorita?*"

Teresa looked at the rest of the group. Although Teresa had an ancestor from Mexico, which gave her slightly

Latina features, Marina knew she didn't speak Spanish. They'd joked about how many times she'd been mistaken for a local on the trip because of her looks.

The group stopped. The teen stepped forward again and held the bag open and motioned to Teresa. He'd been polite with his initial "Excuse me, miss" but there was something about the look in his eyes that Marina didn't like.

"Quiere tortugas?"

"Oh no! He wants to know if we want to buy turtle products," Marina whispered.

Simon stepped forward. "No! *Mal!*"

Marina smiled at his basic "No! Bad!" He'd picked up enough Spanish to get his point across. The teens waved them on and walked back to their shaded spot in the brush. Marina watched them go. She thought she saw something in the bag move.

"Wait! Maybe it's alive," she said.

The teens heard her and walked back to the group of students. This time they headed to Marina.

"Quiere?" the boy asked again.

"Do I want it? Is it alive or not? *Vive o muerto?*"

The boy broke out in a grin. He pulled one of the struggling turtles from the bags. It was only a foot or so long, not a fully mature adult.

"Ah, ess okay! *Tortugas estan bien!*"

Everyone rushed over.

"This is great. We can bring them to the center," said Kristen.

"No. Look." Ryan pointed down the beach.

A small boat was secured there by an anchor. Marina recognized the familiar red, green, and yellow paint immediately.

"Donde es el dinero?" The teen rubbed his fingers together in the universal sign for money.

"They want money for them?" Simon looked confused.

Link nodded and pulled Marina away. "Marco told us about this. They're poachers. We have to go."

"They'll just keep doing it," Ryan said, "which means more turtles will get hurt. They'll recapture them and sell them again. And when they are big enough, they'll kill them anyway."

"It's like Marco said, we have to stop the demand," Marina said.

Kristen gave the turtle a last sad look and let her boyfriend pull her away.

"Wait." Ryan was pulling out his wallet.

"Marina, can you ask them if I can pay them to take a picture of it—a picture of all the turtles they have."

Marina didn't see why anyone would want a photograph of such a sad thing.

"Please?" he implored.

Marina stepped forward. She wasn't exactly sure how

to say it, but she tried. *"Um, dinero por la fotografía de las tortugas?"*

The boys grinned, laughing at their luck. They accepted the bills and pulled the burlap aside to show the other two turtles. The biggest one was almost a foot and a half long. The smiling trio moved in together and held the three turtles for Ryan's shot. Ryan focused in on the turtles, then raised his lens and clicked.

Chapter Nineteen

The morning of the good-bye party, Marina woke up early. Since Marco had commended them for not falling into the trap of bargaining with the turtle poachers the day before, she had slept soundly. But she didn't want to waste a single minute of her last day abroad. She couldn't believe they'd be leaving to go back to Miami in the wee hours of the next morning. The boat was going to start its new position as the Dominican Republic *Tiburon*, and they would head on to their individual futures, too. She wasn't ready to say good-bye to her friends, to the boat, to the island, and especially to Link.

Marina stared out the porthole at the morning sun sparkling on the water. Before she began this semester, she knew she wanted to live her life near the sea. But, after this trip, she felt the islands in her blood, too. The University of Hawaii was far from her family in Vermont, but the CD they sent of the beautiful campus proved that it was just the island for her. Hawaii was only a plane ride away from Vermont. And Australia was only a plane ride away from Hawaii. It was something she had repeated in her head quite a few times during the past few days. She was never going to change her life for a guy again. But it was a nice bonus that her guy lived on the biggest ocean reef in the world.

Marina stood up and woke Jeanette. Together they went down and grabbed coffees for the guys before going to wake them. They had all made a pact that the first one up would wake the others. No one wanted to miss out on a single minute of this day. Si and Kris were already practically melded into each other in the lounge. They'd decided not to crash at all the previous night. Marina felt the tears sting at the sight of Simon clinging so tight to Kristen.

"They look so miserable," she whispered to Jeanette.

"Well, they've already been through the separation thing once."

"I know. It must be awful."

"No. I mean, they've already been through the separation thing, and here they are. Together."

• • •

Later that afternoon, the minibus brought them through the crowded streets of Marco's mother's neighborhood. The houses had a feel of history about them, and, to Marina, even the run-down look of peeling paint added character. She smiled through the window at all the kids wandering free, playing under the watchful eyes of the community. Bright green leaves adorned the trees outside of Marco's mother's small house. As everyone filed off the bus and into the shade, Marco greeted each of his family members warmly. Marina noted his huge smile, and she couldn't imagine how hard it must be for him, having lived away from them for so long.

Marco's family was friendly and welcoming, and before long, their group was all smiling and laughing along with Marco. Music played from an old boombox, and Tali and Teresa danced with some of Marco's cousins. Marina stood in the yard, chewing the sweet candylike juice out of a chunk of sugarcane, waiting for her turn on the coconut grater. The hard flesh of the coconuts was being shredded and would be pressed with water to make coconut cream. Her arm got tired after about six strokes, but the family gathered around cheering Link on as he tirelessly ground the coconut flesh against the homemade metal grater. She'd smiled at the weird sense of pride she felt at Link's coconut-shredding abilities. She never anticipated that that would have been on her list of attractive qualities in a guy.

Marco's mother finished boiling the coconut cream, and ladled it over fresh snapper that Marco's brothers had caught earlier that day. Their group combined with Marco's family, filling the cozy concrete and tin-roofed home. They sat in white plastic lawn chairs or on the patio with their plates on their laps. The cool cement felt good on Marina's legs, and the local food was the best she'd had yet.

Everything was perfect. But looking around at Marco's family and all her boat mates, the sadness of leaving began to sink in again. Somewhere in these last two months, her new friends had become like family to her. And even though she couldn't wait to see her parents, she felt like she'd be leaving another part of her family behind. She glanced at Marco, who was sitting next to his mother, and realized he'd be leaving his family, too. How did he do it?

Link slid in next to Marina on the ground, and put his arm around her. She shivered at how good that felt. He pulled her in closer, and they smiled at each other as Marco called them all to attention.

Marco thanked his family, then readied their group for the bus back to the boat. In twelve hours they'd all be flying together to Miami before heading their separate ways. Link must have caught her look of despair at the thought. He squeezed her hand and leaned against her.

"We'll make it work, Barbie," he whispered.

Marina didn't trust herself to speak, so she just nodded and tried to swallow past the knot in her throat.

Back at the boat, Marco bonged the dive bell a final time. The sound brought a small tremor of moans and stifled sobs through the close-knit group.

"Hello, everyone. I want first to thank you for joining my family at our home. I hope you all enjoyed the *típico* meal," Marco started.

Everyone clapped.

"Well, guys. I don't know what to say." Marco's voice was rough with emotion. "When I signed on for this, I had no idea what great people you all would be. You've just really made this the best experience for me."

There was a sprinkling of applause among the loud sniffles.

"I'm going to miss each and every one of you. I know many of you have made lifelong friends, and, despite the distance you might find between you, one thing you can take away from this semester is that the world is a small place."

Ryan and Jeanette smiled at each other. Ryan's town in Canada was only about three hours north of Detroit. So Jeanette could see him all summer when she lived with her mom. They had already made plans to visit and to keep an open mind about the future. Marina tried not to feel jealous. Link pulled her closer. He kissed her forehead as she snuggled against his chest.

"I wish that I could give every one of you what you deserve. But as it is, I'd like at least to congratulate two of you on your achievements during our trip, and award you the *Tiburon* academic prize," Marco said.

There was a murmur through the group.

"This student impressed me early with the quality of her essays and understanding of the places and people we visited. Her dedication in the field was shown not only by saving the life of a baby dolphin, but Captain Ron assures me she scraped more gunk off the bottom of a boat than a whale shark would eat in a year. Marina!"

Marina couldn't believe it; she had won! She had hoped, but she hadn't been sure, and the announcement seemed so quick that she was afraid to stand up in case she heard wrong. Marco smiled and hugged her as she finally stood to accept the folder with her award details.

Jeanette was jumping up and down and whoo-hooing, and Marina allowed herself to be silly and joined her in the jumping before sitting back down. Link hugged her hard, and a bittersweet pang hit her. Even though they'd been working together in the Dominican Republic to earn TripTask points, she knew he hadn't done much in Utila, and her fantasies of their bubbling up in their dive gear next to marine iguanas and tortoises were slipping away.

She might have saved the baby dolphin, but Link had saved her. Her disappointment must have shown, but Link seemed surprisingly unconcerned.

"And the student with the second highest point total wasn't always obvious about his work performed in the field. With strong essays and creative ideas toward earning points, he showed his dedication to the people of the islands. In learning about their culture, and in particular his tireless work and efforts in rebuilding the Mariposa children's art studio and gallery on the island of—"

"Utila," Marina breathed in wonder.

She stared up at Link as he stood to accept the other prize. He looked down at her and winked.

She was finally getting used to that.

"See, Barbie? What'd I tell ya?"

He laughed, and she smacked him before yanking him down and kissing him. He kissed her back before laughing again.

"Galápagos?" Link asked.

"Galápagos!"

Everyone laughed, and it took Marco a while to get them settled back once more.

"Okay, okay. I think it is only fitting for your last act on this boat to be one symbolic of your own journey and the start of a new chapter in your future."

Marco turned and brought a large box from the kitchen area.

"I've had these guys checked out, and the scientist at the center agreed that they were very lucky turtles. Thanks to some quick thinking on Ryan's part, he was able to snap a photo to identify the kids involved in the poaching. I brought Ryan's photograph of the teenagers to the local head of the village. Kids here have a lot of respect for their elders, and, thanks to that, the culprits surrendered the turtles immediately. I hope while using their boat with the turtle refuge facility for community service, they will come to appreciate the animals for more than profit. It's really kind of a miracle. Ryan, you've made a real difference here. And I think that you should have the honor of releasing them back into the wild."

He presented the box to a red-faced Ryan. Ryan shrugged away the applause and cheers and headed toward the back deck of the boat. He turned back to his friends still sitting at the booth.

"Hey. Would you guys like to help me?"

The six filed out, laughing and hugging. They lined up on the back deck. Ryan carefully lifted out one turtle and put it in Kristen's hands. Simon put one arm around her. He helped steady the turtle with the other and led her to the water's edge. Ryan lifted another into Marina's hands. She peeked at Link from under her lashes, suddenly feeling shy. The feeling floated away as she felt the warmth of his hand meet hers on the back of the turtle. They took their spot next to Si and Kris. Ryan handed the last turtle to

a grinning Jeanette, then trailed after her and knelt down beside the others.

"Look at the sun," Marina breathed.

It dipped with the lower edge seeming to touch the surface of the ocean. The sky was shot through with purple and orange streaks. They smiled at one another and waited for just the right moment. Marina stared at the edge of the horizon and, at the last possible moment, gave a small nod. Marina smiled as the three turtles slid into the ocean with the setting sun.